ANTHONY PARSON

Take Me Home

First published by THE LIICO COMPANY 2025

This novel is entirely a work of fiction. The names, characters and incidents portrayed in it are the work of the author's imagination. Any resemblance to actual persons, living or dead, events or localities is entirely coincidental.

Anthony Parson asserts the moral right to be identified as the author of this work.

First edition

ISBN: 979-8-218-66212-7

Library of Congress Control Number (LCCN): 2025908694

Email: liicosoundstudio@gmail.com

To the ones who hide in pages
Who find themselves in fractured stages
To every soul that seeks escape
through fiction's warm, forgiving shape
And to the rhythm once in reach
A tempo lost between each sheet
You were the hum beneath my skin
A storm in swing, a pulse within
No spotlight, name, or final bow
Just silence where there once was sound
But still your echo moves the pen—
A quiet jazz I write again
This book began where music stopped
Where something beautiful was suddenly dropped

"Reality is not a place.
It's a sentence."

Anthony Parson

Contents

1

The Weight of Words

The rain drummed lightly against the window-pane, a rhythmic tapping that filled the silence of her dimly lit apartment. Books lined the walls, their spines worn and faded, each one a testament to the years she had spent lost in worlds that weren't her own. Once, those stories had poured from her like an unstoppable river, her words shaping realities that captivated millions. Now, the river had dried up, leaving her stranded in the desert of her own mind. Marisa Cole, once a bestselling author, now spent most of her days circling the ghost of an idea that never fully formed. She had tried everything—writing exercises, meditation, therapy, even sex—but the words would not come. It had been two years since her last novel, and the silence in her head had grown deafening.

She exhaled, rubbing her temples as she stared

at the blank document on her laptop screen. The cursor blinked, taunting her. Her agent had stopped calling months ago, her publisher had quietly moved on, and the industry that once celebrated her had barely noticed her absence. She knew what they whispered: *One-hit wonder. Burnt out. Cooked. Lost her magic.* Marisa closed the laptop with a sigh. Her fingers twitched for something, anything to break the monotony of failure. Writing had always been her escape, her way of making sense of the world. Without it, she felt lost, scared as if she were drifting in a sea of static. In a sense she felt like dying.

Her therapist had suggested she find new ways to reconnect with herself, to rediscover joy in the mundane. *Get out of the apartment,* she had said. *Do something that makes you feel alive.* Marisa wasn't sure what that was anymore. But she did know one thing: she needed a book. Not to write, but to read. Something to remind her why stories mattered in the first place. She glanced around the apartment, her gaze settling on the stacks of books by her bedside. They had become monuments to her avoidance. She had devoured them in a frenzy, one after another, as if losing herself in other people's words would somehow rekindle her own. But it hadn't. The stories had been a temporary balm, numbing her mind and keeping her demons at bay. Lately, even that escape was losing its power.

A memory stirred—her debut novel's launch party. A whirlwind night of champagne and flashing cameras. She had stood at the center of it all, smiling while her mind raced with doubts. What if this is the best I'll ever do? The answer had come silently over the years, a slow, suffocating decline of inspiration. With a sigh, she grabbed her coat and keys. Maybe a new story is what I need.

Marisa's love affair with words had begun long before the world knew her name. As a child, she had found solace in books, escaping into stories where endings could be rewritten, where broken things could be made whole again. Her mother had always worked late, and her father had left when she was six. His absents left her with permanent scars. Books became her refuge, her escape from a world that often felt too big and too empty. When she was ten, she started writing her own stories, scribbling them in spiral notebooks with frayed edges. Her stories were her secret world, one where she controlled the chaos. She remembered one in particular—a tale about a girl who could speak to shadows. It had been raw and messy, but it was hers. Her mother had stumbled upon that notebook one night.

Marisa had expected praise or curiosity. Instead, her mother had looked worried. "Why do you write such dark things, honey?" Marisa hadn't known how to answer. She just knew that writing made the emptiness feels less consuming. As her talent grew, her stories became more polished. By the time she was sixteen, she had won her first writing competition. Her mother had been proud then, her worries buried beneath the applause of strangers. But even then, Marisa had felt the weight of expectation settle over her.

Her debut novel, *Echoes of Yesteryear*, had catapulted her into the spotlight. She was only twenty-one when the book topped bestseller lists. Critics hailed her as the next great literary voice, and publishers scrambled for her next manuscript. But success had a price. The more the world demanded of her, the less she felt in control. The pressure to produce, to exceed expectations, grew suffocating. Each book had to be bigger, better, grand. And with each one, she felt herself slipping further from the joy that had once fueled her writing.

Her relationships suffered. Her mother, who had once been her biggest supporter, grew distant. Friends drifted away, unable to understand the isolation that came with success. Even love had been fleeting—her last relationship crumbling under the weight of her self-imposed exile. She had sacrificed everything for her stories. And now, those stories had abandoned her. And so, she found herself stepping into the small thrift shop on the corner of Grove and Pine.

The bell above the door chimed as she entered, the scent of old paper and worn leather wrapping around her like an embrace. The store was nearly empty, only having a young clerk at the counter who barely glanced up from his phone. The place was a mess, as always—piles of books stacked haphazardly, forgotten trinkets gathering dust on wooden shelves. Marisa had been coming here for years. She liked the way stories lingered in secondhand books, the way they carried echoes of past readers. There was something comforting about knowing she wasn't the first person to hold a particular book, that someone else had once found comfort within its pages.

She wandered past the usual sections—mystery, romance, science fiction—letting her fingers trail along the spines, humming a beautiful song. Nothing called to her. Everything felt like blah, as she would put it. Not until she reached the back corner of the store. The back corner was different. The light seemed dimmer there, the air heavier, and the dusk was thicker. It was the part of the store most customers ignored, a forgotten space filled with oddities that didn't quite fit. Similar to how Marisa felt in society. Alone, forgotten and awkward in a world filled with movement. Old photographs in cracked frames, porcelain dolls with chipped faces, and furniture that had seen better days.

A single chair sat beside the old wooden table, half-cast in the shadows of the dimly lit room. At first glance, it looked utterly ordinary—unremarkable in every way. The frame was wooden, its edges softened by time, the kind of smooth wear that only comes from years of use. Faint scratches lined its legs like forgotten stories, and one of the back spindles leaned ever so slightly, as if tired from holding too many secrets. Its seat, a once-rich leather, had faded to a dusty brown, cracked and weathered like dry earth. The material sagged just slightly in the center, shaped by the weight of countless visitors long gone. It didn't creak when she touched it—no dramatic signs of menace. But still, something about it gave her pause. Not fear exactly, but awareness. A quiet sense that it was watching, waiting, even though it hadn't moved an inch.

It was the kind of chair people passed by without a second thought. Overlooked. Forgotten. But standing in front of it now, she couldn't shake the feeling that it was anything but ordinary. "You like it?" She turned to see an older woman standing nearby, her gray hair pulled into a loose bun. Marisa had never seen her before, which was odd—she thought she knew all the employees here. "It's just a chair," Marisa said with a small shrug. The woman smiled. "That's what most people think." She ran a hand along the table's surface. "The man who brought it in said it belonged to his family for generations. Said it had... history." "History?" "Stories, really," the woman said, almost to herself. Her eyes took on a distant look, as if recalling something long forgotten. "Some objects... they carry the weight of the lives that touched them. This chair has been a witness to many stories."

Marisa felt a chill dance along her skin, but she couldn't tear her gaze away. "What happened to the family?" The woman's eyes sharpened, her distant expression vanishing. "He was the last of them. No one left to inherit." Marisa frowned. "And he just gave it away?" "He said it was time," the woman replied softly, her voice barely above a whisper. Marisa hesitated. The whole conversation felt strange—like she had stepped into a story rather than real life. But something about the chair called to her. As if it were waiting. As if it had chosen her.

Slowly, she sat down. The moment her body sank into the worn fabric, a shiver ran up her spine. It wasn't unpleasant, but it was... unfamiliar. Like the whisper of something forgotten brushing against the edges of her mind. Her fingertips grazed the table beside her, and for a fleeting moment, an image flashed in her mind—a room she didn't recognize, filled with flickering candlelight and the scent of something old and earthy. The vision was gone as quickly as it came, leaving behind a lingering unease.

Marisa blinked, her heart pounding in her ears. She

glanced around, half-expecting to see something out of place. But the store was the same. Only the chair and the table remained, waiting. She stayed longer than she intended, her fingers lightly tracing the edges of the scratches. Something about those faint lines stirred something deep inside her—a feeling she hadn't experienced in years. Marisa's chest tightened. What if this was her chance? Not just to write again, but to reclaim the part of herself she had lost. Her mind raced with possibilities.

Maybe this was the push she needed. Maybe it was fate. Or maybe—just maybe—it was time to stop running. As she stood, her gaze lingered on the chair one last time. The air around her felt heavier, charged with something she couldn't quite name.

At the counter, Marisa placed the chair and table carefully by the counter. The young employee behind the register, a boy who looked no older than nineteen, gave her a curious glance. "Nice find," he said, scanning the price tag. "Not many people take an interest in the stuff from the back corner." The boy was new so he didn't know that Marisa always shops from the back corner. She tells him that, that's where the best stuff lives. Marisa offered a faint smile. "Something about it just… felt right."

The boy nodded knowingly. "Yeah, that happens sometimes." He leaned in slightly, lowering his voice as if sharing a secret. "You know, the guy who

brought this in... he had a story about that chair."
Marisa's interest piqued. "What kind of story?" The
boy's expression grew thoughtful. "An older man—
he was 88, I think—came in yesterday. Said the chair
had been in his family for generations. He inherited
it from his great-grandmother. He told me it was...
special." "Special how?" Marisa asked, her anxiety
grew. The boy shrugged, but his eyes gleamed with
curiosity. "He said it was magical... but not in a weird,
spooky way. More like... sentimental magic. Like
the kind of magic you feel when something has been
loved for a long time."

Marisa's fingers tightened around the edge of the
table. "And he just... gave it away?" "He said it was
time," the boy replied softly, echoing the words of
the older woman Marisa had spoken to earlier. "He
wanted it to go to someone who would appreciate
it. Someone who needed it." Marisa's throat felt
dry. "Did he say anything else?" The boy thought
for a moment, then shook his head. "Just that he
hoped whoever took it would take care of it. Like his
family had." Marisa felt the weight of the chair and
table in her hands grow heavier, as if the stories they
carried were settling onto her shoulders. "Thank
you," as she expressed gratitude, her voice barely
above a whisper.

The boy smiled as he placed the receipt in her hand.
"Hope it brings you something good, we will delivery

9

it by tomorrow evening." As Marisa walked out of the shop, the weight of the chair seemed to press deeper into her palms. But for the first time in years, she didn't mind the weight. In fact, she welcomed it. She didn't yet know it, but this story would change everything.

2

The Seat of Something Strange

T he chair and table had become part of her space, blending seamlessly into the quiet sanctuary of her home library. Days had passed since the chair and table was delivered to her home, and though they fit perfectly into the room—nestled in the corner beneath the soft glow of a floor lamp—Marisa hadn't been able to bring herself to sit in the chair. At first, she told herself she was simply too busy, caught up in her usual routine of avoiding writing and losing herself in the comfort of old stories. But as the days stretched on, an inexplicable tension settled over her whenever she glanced at the chair. It was as if the chair was waiting—patient, silent, but somehow expectant. The scent of aged paper and ink filled the room, mingling with the faint musk of the chair's worn fabric. Her library was her refuge, a place where stories lived and breathed, but lately, even here, she couldn't shake the feeling that something had shifted.

Every time she passed by the chair, that strange unease curled in her stomach—a quiet, insistent tug at the edges of her awareness. She tried to ignore it, dismiss it as exhaustion or overactive imagination. But the feeling lingered, growing stronger each day. Tonight was different. Tonight, she couldn't ignore it anymore. Her library was her sanctuary—a small, cozy space filled with shelves of books that had shaped her life. The scent of aged paper and ink lingered in the air, wrapping around her like an old friend. But even here, surrounded by the stories that had once brought her comfort, she felt an unease she couldn't explain. She hadn't been able to bring herself to sit in it yet—though she wasn't sure why. Every time she glanced at the chair, a strange unease developed in her stomach, like a distant memory tugging at the edges of her mind.

After hours of sitting in front of her laptop, the cursor blinked back at her, mocking her silence. Her thoughts felt heavy, tangled in the fog that had clouded her mind for months. She had tried everything—music, candles, even reading old favorite passages—but nothing worked. With a sigh, Marisa stood, stretching her arms overhead. Her eyes drifted toward the chair. Maybe I just need a change of scenery. Grabbing the paperback novel that had been collecting dust on her coffee table, she walked over and sat down. The fabric was cool against her skin, the worn texture familiar yet unfamiliar. She leaned back, sinking into the chair as she flipped the book open to where she had left off.

It was a slasher novel—raw and unforgiving, the kind that bled tension from every page. The story gripped her from the start, gritty and relentless, the way those dog-eared paperbacks used to when she was a teenager hiding under the covers with a flashlight. The protagonist was a weathered detective, hollowed out by years of chasing monsters, now hunting a killer who moved like smoke through the city's decaying heart. The streets in the book were as broken as the people who wandered them—cracked concrete, dim-lit bars, whispered threats hiding in every shadow.

Marisa sank into the words, letting the pulse of the story tether itself to her own. The room around her softened, faded. She barely noticed the time slipping by. Her eyes followed each line with hungry focus, her imagination sketching out scenes in sharp detail—narrow alleyways swallowed by darkness, flickering streetlights overhead, the sharp slap of footsteps behind you when you're sure you're alone.

And then—everything changed.

The warm glow of her living room lamp stuttered

and vanished, replaced by a sickly wash of neon light that blinked above her head like a dying heartbeat. The smell hit her first—wet asphalt, engine fumes, and something metallic beneath it all. The familiar silence of her apartment gave way to the low hum of distant traffic, punctuated by a far-off siren wailing like a warning. Her breath caught. This wasn't the book anymore. She was in it.

Marisa heart race as she realized... She wasn't in her living room anymore. She was standing in an alley. Her breath trapped in her throat like a hostage as she turned, taking in her surroundings. The crumbling brick walls, the dripping water from a nearby fire escape, the eerie silence that pressed down on her—everything matched the scene she had just read. Marisa's pulse quickened. She spun around, her eyes darting across the darkness. The air was thick, heavy with the promise of danger. Her mind screamed at her to move, but her body felt frozen in place. A shadow shifted in the distance. Footsteps echoed off the damp pavement. "No," she whispered, her voice barely audible. But the footsteps grew louder, closer. Panic clawed at her throat as her mind scrambled for an explanation. "This has to be a dream."

She squeezed her eyes shut, fists clenched at her sides, as if sheer will alone could pull her out of whatever twisted dream this was. *Wake up*, she pleaded silently. *Wake up.* But the world didn't fade. Instead, it sharpened. The scrape of boots against gritty pavement echoed closer, louder, every step a threat she couldn't see. The alley stretched with an oppressive stillness, the distant hum of the city pressing in like a slow breath on the back of her neck. Her heart thundered in her chest, drowning out reason. *Say something. Do something.* "God... take me home," she whispered, barely louder than a breath. Her voice trembled, brittle as glass.

For a single, agonizing heartbeat—nothing. And then—The air cracked. A low tremor passed through her bones, as if reality itself had stuttered. The alley buckled, edges blurring like smeared ink. A wave of vertigo crashed over her, and the sharp scent of damp concrete evaporated all at once, replaced by the faint aroma of old books, lavender candles, and the quiet hum of a nearby heater. Warm light poured across her closed eyelids. She opened her eyes. She was back—her living room exactly as she'd left it. But something inside her had shifted. She could feel it in her chest, in her breath. Whatever that was... it wasn't just a dream.

Sitting in the chair. The novel lay open in her lap, the words on the page blurring together as her hands trembled. Her breathing came in short, ragged gasps. Sweat beaded on her forehead, and her pulse thundered in her ears. Marisa's mind struggling to make sense of what had just happened. Was that real? Her eyes scanned the room, half-expecting to see remnants of the alley lingering in the shadows. But everything was normal. The soft glow of her lamp, the faint hum of the refrigerator, the quiet stillness of her apartment. "Just a dream," she mumbled, her voice barely above a whisper. But even as she spoke the words aloud, they felt hollow. Her fingers grazed the edges of the book, her grip tightening. It felt too real. Her mind raced, trying to rationalize what had happened.

Maybe she had dozed off while reading—gotten lost in the story so deeply that her mind had conjured a vivid dream, the kind that clings to your skin long after waking. That would've made sense. A dream. Just a dream. But that didn't explain the sharp scent of damp pavement still lingering in her nose, or the distant echo of footsteps that seemed to reverberate in her chest like a fading memory. It didn't explain the pounding in her veins, the way her fingers trembled slightly, as if she'd been running for her life only moments ago.

Marisa swallowed hard. Her throat burned, dry and scraped raw like she'd been screaming into nothing. Her gaze drifted downward, landing on the chair beneath her. It looked ordinary—wooden frame, worn leather seat, the kind of thing someone might glance at once and forget. Faded, scuffed, a little crooked. There was nothing outwardly strange about it. Nothing that hinted at what had just happened. But something wasn't right. The room around her was quiet. Too quiet. Not peaceful, but *unnatural*—like the air itself had thickened, pressing in around her, listening. The light hadn't changed, and yet it felt dimmer somehow, like the walls were holding back a secret. Her skin prickled. Her pulse hadn't slowed.

The chair hadn't moved. It hadn't changed. But the world felt different now. Like she'd stepped back into her life—but not quite the same one she'd left. For a long moment, she didn't move. She just sat there, listening to the echo of her heartbeat slowing in her ears, trying to convince herself that she hadn't actually felt the rain on her skin or heard the stranger's voice whispering her name. That she hadn't really been there. But even as her body began to calm, her mind churned with a restless energy. Thoughts collided in her head, chaotic and sharp. One thing kept rising above the noise, pushing through all doubt like a splinter in her consciousness—clear, cold, undeniable. That was no ordinary dream.

3

A Dangerous Escape

Two days had passed since Marisa's terrifying experience with the chair, but the memory hadn't faded. If anything, it lingered, growing sharper and more vivid with each passing hour. The feeling of the damp pavement beneath her feet, the echo of footsteps in the alley, the cold grip of fear—it was all still there, etched into her mind. She had tried to dismiss it. Tried to convince herself that it had been nothing more than an overactive imagination or a vivid dream. But deep down, she knew better. Something had happened. Something real. And the chair was at the center of it.

Marisa had avoided the library since that night, but the pull was too strong. Her curiosity gnawed at her, refusing to be silenced. She needed answers. On the third night, unable to resist any longer, she returned to her library. The chair and table sat exactly where she had left them, bathed in the soft glow of the floor lamp. She hesitated, her heart pounding as she approached. Her fingers brushed the edge of the table, and a chill ran down her spine. That's when she saw it. The words. Etched faintly into the surface of the table, barely visible beneath the scratches and worn finish, were three words: Take Me Home.

Marisa's breath caught in her throat. Her fingers traced the letters, her mind racing. "take me home." The words she had whispered in panic when she had been trapped in that alley. Could it be? Her mind spun as she tried to make sense of it. What if... No. It was impossible. And yet... The memory was too vivid, too real. Her pulse increases as she pieced it together—the chair, the book, the alley, and then the words that had brought her back. Take Me Home. A wave of unease washed over her. If the words had the power to bring her back, what else could the chair do? Marisa's thoughts raced, her mind a whirlwind of questions with no answers. But one thing was certain: She had to find out.

The next night, Marisa couldn't resist. The pull of the chair was too strong. She needed to know if it had truly happened—or if her mind was playing tricks on her. This time, she chose a different book. Something less intense, less terrifying. A historical romance, light and familiar. If she was going to test the chair; she wanted to do it somewhere safe.

Her hands trembled as she sat down, the familiar coolness of the fabric sending a shiver through her body. She opened the book, her eyes scanning the words. The world around her shifted. It wasn't as jarring as the first time. This time, she was ready—or at least as ready as she could be.

Marisa world had changed again. She stood in the center of a grand ballroom, its vaulted ceiling soaring high above, draped in silk and flickering candlelight. The air was overtaken by the heady perfume of roses, warm and intoxicating. Laughter rang out like crystal, delicate and distant, navigating through the elegant waltz playing from a string quartet in the far corner. Gowns in every color spun across the marble floor, their jeweled hems catching the light like fire. Her heart pounded, but this time, it wasn't terror that held her still. It was wonder.

She took a slow, cautious step forward. Her shoes clicked gently against the polished floor, each sound swallowed by the swell of music and movement. Everything was impossibly vivid—the glint of a diamond earring, the flutter of a fan, the gold-leaf molding on the distant walls. It was beautiful. Too beautiful. Then it hit her—*this* was the world of the book. Somehow, impossibly, she was inside it. Her breath caught, panic bubbling just beneath the surface, but she didn't let it take her. Instead, she exhaled slowly, steadying herself, and whispered the words, barely more than a breath: "Take me home." And just like that—The ballroom vanished. Light shifted. Air rushed back into her lungs. The scent of roses dissolved, replaced by the faint aroma of dust and fabric softener. The music faded into silence. She was back. But the pacing of her heart told her nothing about this was over.

Marisa's heart thundered in her chest as she sat frozen in the chair, the book still splayed open in her lap. Her breaths came fast and shallow, her thoughts racing, spiraling through a thousand impossible questions. But one truth pulsed louder than all the rest—it wasn't a dream. The chair was real. And it had power. In the days that followed, sleep became an afterthought. Curiosity turned to obsession. She couldn't stay away. Each night, with trembling hands and a jumpy heart, Marisa eased herself into the seat. The leather, cracked and cool, seemed to pulse with quiet energy beneath her.

She wandered through enchanted forests where creatures whispered in forgotten tongues. She scaled frozen peaks above cloud-covered kingdoms, her breath catching with wonder. She walked the gas-lit streets of Victorian London, fog grabbing at her heels, secrets hiding behind every door. She stumbled through scorched wastelands where the sky bled orange, and survival was etched into every face she passed. Each time, the chair carried her there.

Each time, she came back. The line between fiction and reality blurred a little more with every journey. Books were no longer stories—they were places. And the chair... the chair had become her escape. Her sanctuary. Her addiction.

When the weight of her failure pressed down on her, when the silence of her empty apartment became too much to bear, she sought refuge in the stories. The chair offered her a way out—an escape from the guilt, the loneliness, the crushing feeling of inadequacy. But with each journey, the line between reality and fiction blurred a little more. And though Marisa reveled in the escape, a small voice whispered at the back of her mind. Be careful. Because magic— especially magic tied to stories—always came with a price.

At first, it was easy to explain away. The chair gave her something she hadn't felt in years—purpose, thrill, wonder. Each journey lit a fire in her veins, stirred something long buried beneath the dull rhythm of her everyday life. It was more than just adventure now. It was connection. Discovery. Even love. Somewhere out there, between the inked lines of fantasy and fiction, she had found what reality had stolen from her. But as days blurred into weeks, the cracks began to show. It started small. A faint dizziness when she returned, like jet lag from a place no map could find. A sluggishness that clung to her thoughts, making the real world feel slow and unreal, like she was moving through water. And then came the dreams.

They arrived uninvited—vivid, jarring flashes of places she'd visited: glowing forests, burning cities, quiet, rain-soaked streets. Faces she'd spoken to in fiction turned toward her in sleep, whispering things she couldn't quite remember upon waking. The dreams bled into waking hours, too. Sometimes she'd glance at a stranger and swear she recognized them from a story. Sometimes, she didn't recognize herself. But she brushed it all aside. The chair was helping her. That's what she told herself when the room felt like it was tilting. When the days started to lose shape. When reality no longer felt like the safest place to be. Because admitting something was wrong... meant stopping. And Marisa wasn't ready to stop. Not yet. Because deep down, she knew—She wasn't just escaping the world.

4

The Price of Passage

Marisa's experiments with the chair had become a routine—an escape she both feared and craved. But with each passing journey, she began to notice patterns. It started subtly. A feeling of familiarity when she returned. The scent of roses from the ballroom lingering long after she had whispered the words "Take me home." Or the gritty sensation of sand between her toes after a journey to a desert wasteland. At first, she chalked it up to her imagination, a side effect of immersing herself so deeply in the stories. But then the effects became harder to ignore.

The voices came softly at first. Barely there—like whispers caught in the wind, brushing against the edges of her thoughts. Marisa barely noticed them in the beginning, chalking them up to imagination or leftover dream residue. But they didn't fade. They grew. With each journey through the chair, the voices sharpened. Clearer. Louder. Characters she had met, places she had wandered—*they remembered her*. Their words echoed in her mind at odd hours, sometimes in the hush between thoughts, other times so suddenly they made her flinch. What had once been stories confined to pages now lived on inside her. They weren't fading when she returned. They were following her back.

Marisa tried to explain it away. She told herself it was normal, expected even. Her mind was adapting, adjusting to the intensity of the experiences. It was a psychological echo, that's all. Immersion hangover. But deep down, she knew better. This wasn't imagination. It was *residue*. Something was changing in her. Or around her. The boundary between what was real and what was written had thinned—and maybe, just maybe, it was breaking. Then, after one particularly brutal journey—a dive into a dystopian thriller filled with violence and moral decay—Marisa stumbled across something that made her blood run cold. A detail that didn't belong. Not in the book. Not in her world. And certainly not in *both*.

Marisa had returned from a bleak, desolate future where the world had been consumed by war and technology. She had spent hours navigating through that world, narrowly escaping danger at every turn.

When she whispered "Take me home," she had felt the familiar pull, the sudden shift that brought her back to the safety of her library. But as her breathing steadied and her mind cleared, her eyes fell to the table. The words "Take Me Home" stood out starkly against the worn surface, but beneath them— faint, almost as if hidden by time—were more words. "What you read... becomes real." Marisa's heart skipped a beat.

Her fingers hovered over the words, then slowly traced the letters carved into the edge of the chair— words she had never noticed before, hidden in the worn grain of the wood like a secret waiting to be found. *What you read becomes real.* The phrase struck her like a freight train, slamming through her and stealing the breath from her lungs. It *wasn't* just in her head. None of it. The rose-scented air, the slick feel of rain-slick pavement beneath her boots, the lingering cadence of voices that didn't belong to this world—they hadn't faded because they weren't memories. They were *imprints*. Ghosts of the lives she'd stepped into. Realities she had touched. Lived.

Marisa's hands began to tremble. The room spun slightly as the enormity of it settled over her, as if the walls themselves leaned in to listen. She grabbed her laptop with fumbling fingers, dragging it across the table like a lifeline. She began to write with fumbling fingers. Frantic, messy thoughts spilled onto the page—half sentences, fragmented questions, raw theories. She had to *understand.* Had to piece this together before it slipped too far out of reach. This was power. And power like this always came with a cost

Over the next few days, Marisa conducted tests. She chose shorter books, less immersive, and sat in the chair with careful intent. She stayed in the worlds for shorter periods, observing what lingered when she returned. The first rule became clear: Whatever she read while sitting in the chair became reality—but only until she whispered the words "Take me home." The moment she says, "take me home" the world dissolved, and she was back in her library. The second rule emerged soon after: The longer she stayed in a story, the stronger the imprint it left on her mind. A few minutes inside a lighthearted romance left her with a faint warmth that dissipated quickly. But hours in a horror novel had left her jumpy for days, the sounds of footsteps and distant screams echoing in her ears long after she had returned. And then came the most unsettling discovery.

Time in the chair wasn't the same as time in reality. Marisa had noticed it after one particularly long session—a deep exploration into a sprawling fantasy epic that had felt like days. When she returned, only an hour had passed in the real world. But the longer she stayed in the stories, the more disoriented she became when she returned. Reality felt... thinner. Marisa's mind struggled to adjust, the boundaries between her world and the ones she had visited growing blurry.

Marisa couldn't stop. Despite the unease clawing at her mind, despite the growing disorientation, she pushed the boundaries. She wanted to see how far the chair's power went. How much control she had. She ventured deeper into books she wouldn't have dared before—dark, dangerous worlds where survival was never guaranteed. Each time, she pushed herself to stay longer, to immerse herself fully. And each time, she came back with more than just memories. But something was changing.

The voices that whispered in her mind were no longer just echoes. They felt... closer. Stronger. As if the characters she had left behind weren't content to remain where they belonged. And then came the headaches. Blinding pain that struck without warning, leaving her gasping for breath. Flashes of the worlds she had visited danced behind her closed eyelids, too vivid to be ignored. Her mind was struggling to hold onto the boundaries between reality and fiction.

One night, after a particularly intense session, Marisa woke up to the sound of a voice. "You're staying too long." The words were barely a whisper, but they echoed through her mind, chilling her to the core. Marisa sat up, her heart pounding. She glanced around her library, but she was alone. "You're staying too long." The voice came again, softer this time, fading like a distant memory. Her pulse raced. Was it her imagination? A lingering remnant of the worlds she had visited? Or was it... something else? Marisa's mind screamed at her to stop. To leave the chair alone. But she wasn't ready. Not yet. Because despite the warnings, despite the growing fear that something was wrong, Marisa couldn't let go. The chair wasn't just a tool. It was an addiction. And Marisa was too far gone to walk away. But she was about to learn that even magic had its limits. And breaking those limits... came with consequences.

5

In Good Company

It had been months since Marisa last saw Daniel. Her and Daniel's relationship had ended badly, with him blowing up after feeling used by her. He had always created content around her books and her career as an author, pouring his heart into her success. But it became too much for him. He felt that Marisa didn't value what he was doing—he thought that she only took what she needed without giving him a space to express his own creativity. The breaking point came when Daniel had the chance to be her creative producer—a role they had talked about, something he had dreamed of. It was supposed to be his opportunity to finally step out of the shadows and shape their creative vision together. But when the moment came,

Marisa took that opportunity away from him, handing it to someone else. She had stolen the one chance Daniel had to express his own creative vision. Daniel had been coping with the loss of a close relative during that time, someone who had always supported him. The weight of his grief, combined with feeling undervalued by everyone around him, pushed him to the edge. When Marisa denied him that one chance to be the creative producer, everything boiled over. "You used me." Those had been his final words before he walked away, leaving Marisa standing in the wreckage of what they had built together. To Daniel, Marisa had been the only person who truly understood him—until she took that away.

They met at the corner café where the scent of fresh coffee mingled with the hum of quiet conversations. Daniel looked the same— that familiar easy smile that had once made her heart flutter. But there was something different about him too. He seemed... hopeful. "Marisa," he said softly as she slid into the seat across from him. "It's really good to see you." "You too," she murmured, her voice quieter than she intended. The conversation started easily enough— small talk about work, life, and mutual friends. But Daniel's eyes lingered on her, studying her with a quiet intensity that made her stomach twist. "Are you okay?" he asked gently, his brows furrowing. "You seem... different."

Marisa forced a smile. "I've just been busy," she

lied, her mind already drifting back to the chair waiting for her at home. "A lot on my plate." "Yeah?" Daniel's gaze didn't waver. "I've missed you." Her heart clenched. She hadn't expected that. "Maybe... maybe we could try again?" His voice was tentative, filled with a vulnerability that caught her off guard. "I've been thinking about us a lot lately. I don't know, Marisa. I just—" She cut him off with a forced smile, her heart pounding. "Daniel..." "I know," he said quickly, leaning back with a sigh. "I just... I had to ask." Marisa didn't know what to say. Part of her wanted to say yes, to give them another chance. But another part—the part that had been consumed by the chair's magic—knew that she was no longer the woman Daniel had fallen in love with. And she didn't know how to tell him that.

That night, Marisa couldn't stop thinking about Daniel. His words echoed in her mind, tugging at emotions she had tried to bury. But as much as she wanted to believe they could go back to the way things were, she knew they couldn't. But what if... Her gaze drifted toward the chair in the corner of her library. What if she could create a version of Daniel who was perfect? Marisa's heart pounded as the idea took hold. She could write the story of them—the way it should have been.

Before she could stop herself, she was pulling out her notebook, her pen moving feverishly across the page. A love story. Daniel, but better. In this version, he was attentive, understanding, everything she had ever wanted. Their relationship was flawless, their connection unbreakable. There was no distance, no misunderstandings—only perfect harmony. When she was done, Marisa stared at the words on the page, her pulse racing. Without hesitation, she sat down in the chair.

The shift was immediate. One moment, she was in her library. The next, she was standing in a sunlit park, Daniel's hand intertwined with hers. "Marisa," he murmured, his eyes filled with warmth. "I've never been happier." The version of Daniel she had created was everything she had ever dreamed of. He listened. He understood her fears. He supported her dreams without hesitation. The story led them to his car, where they talked about love and marriage, their words laced with unspoken desire. The air grew heavier as the sun dipped below the horizon, the night wrapping around them like a secret.

Daniel's lips found her neck, trailing soft kisses that sent shivers down her spine. A quiet moan escaped her lips as his hands explored her body, sliding beneath her shirt, his touch igniting a fire she hadn't felt in a long time. Her shirt slipped off, and Daniel's mouth was on her skin—hot, hungry, worshiping her. Marisa's breath quickened as her fingers tangled in his hair, pulling him closer. His face pressed against her chest, her body arching into him as heat spread through her veins. They were both lost in the moment, their bodies pressed together, drenched in the heat of their desire. Sweat beaded on their skin as their breaths mingled in the small space of the car. The windows fogged up, the moon hanging high above them, witnessing their passion as it unfolded beneath the cover of night. For a while, time stood still, and Marisa allowed herself to be consumed by the fantasy she had created—a world where Daniel was perfect, and love was exactly as she had written it. And for a while, Marisa allowed herself to believe it was real. But reality was waiting.

When Marisa whispered "Take me home," the perfect world faded, and she was back in her library. But something was... off. The real Daniel wasn't the same. No matter how many times they met for coffee, no matter how hard he tried to rekindle what they had. The disconnect grew wider with each meeting. Daniel noticed her distance, the way her eyes seemed to wander to places he couldn't follow. "Marisa," he said one night, his voice filled with quiet frustration. "Are you even here?" "I'm sorry," she whispered, her gaze distant. But in truth, she wasn't there. Her heart was trapped in a world that wasn't real.

Daniel's patience wore thin. His concern turned to confusion, then to frustration. He asked questions she couldn't answer—where had she been? Why did she seem so far away? Marisa couldn't tell him the truth. Because how could she explain that she had created a version of him that was better than the real thing? And the more she tried to hold onto the illusion, the more she realized... She didn't want Daniel anymore. The man sitting across from her was real, but he wasn't him. The love she had written was perfect. Reality was not.

As the gap between her and Daniel grew, Marisa knew their time was running out. And then, just when she thought she was ready to give up on love altogether... She met him. The CEO. But Marisa didn't know that meeting him would unravel her world even more. And this time... The consequences would be deadly.

6

HIM

Marisa hadn't planned on attending the Art Entertainment Gala. The idea of being surrounded by industry elites, smiling politely while answering questions about a career she had long since abandoned, made her stomach twist. But Emily had insisted. "You need to get out, Marisa," her friend had said, her tone leaving no room for argument. "You can't hide forever." And so, Marisa found herself at the lavish event, the air buzzing with energy and conversation. The ballroom was breathtaking—marble floors reflecting the golden glow of crystal chandeliers, waiters gliding through the crowd with trays of champagne. Yet, despite the grandeur, Marisa felt out of place. She was halfway through her second glass of wine when she noticed him.

Elias Kingston. Tall, confident, and effortlessly

charismatic, Elias commanded attention without even trying. His tailored suit hugged his frame perfectly, and his piercing brown eyes swept the room with quiet authority. Marisa had read about him—a tech mogul turned CEO of a rapidly growing media empire. He was the kind of man who built kingdoms and made fortunes. And now, he was looking at her. Their eyes met across the crowded room, and Marisa felt a spark that caught her off guard. She glanced away, but when she looked back, he was already walking toward her. "Marisa Cole?" His voice was smooth, laced with curiosity and confidence.

Marisa responds with a nervous shake in her voice. "Yes?" "I thought that was you." He offered a warm smile, his eyes holding hers with an intensity that made her breath catch. "I'm Elias Kingston. I'm a big fan of your work." Marisa, caught off guard. "You... you've read my books?" "All of them." His smile deepened, and for a moment, Marisa forgot how to breathe. "You have a remarkable way of bringing stories to life." Heat rose to her cheeks, and she forced herself to stay composed. "Thank you. That means a lot." "May I?" He gestured toward the empty seat beside her. "Of course."

As Elias settled in, their conversation flowed effort- lessly. He was charming without being overbearing, genuinely interested in her work and her thoughts on the industry. Marisa found herself relaxing, drawn to his easy confidence and undeniable magnetism. But she was careful. She kept the conversation light, steering away from anything too personal— especially the chair. The last thing she needed was for Elias to get too close to the truth. Yet, despite her guarded nature, Marisa couldn't deny the growing attraction between them. There was something about Elias that made her feel... alive.

Over the next few weeks, Elias became a constant presence in her life. Their dates were nothing like what she had experienced with Daniel. Elias took her to exclusive restaurants, private art galleries, and spontaneous weekend getaways. He opened doors to a world Marisa had never known—a world of power, luxury, and influence. And Marisa found herself drawn deeper into his orbit. But while Elias swept her off her feet, Marisa couldn't fully let her guard down. The chair was always in the back of her mind. She never mentioned it, never hinted at the truth of what she had discovered. It was her secret, her burden to bear. And as much as she was falling for Elias, she couldn't risk letting him in. Not yet.

Elias, however, was persistent. "You're a mystery, Marisa," he whispered one evening as they strolled through a private garden, moonlight casting a soft glow around them. "I feel like I know pieces of you... but not all of you." Marisa's heart clenched.

She smiled, but it didn't reach her eyes. "Maybe some things are better left unknown." Elias stopped, turning to face her. His gaze was intense, filled with genuine curiosity. "I don't believe that. I think... there's more to you than you're willing to show." For a moment, Marisa considered telling him—about the chair, about the worlds she had created and escaped into. But fear held her back. What if he didn't believe her? Or worse... what if he did?

Marisa swallowed hard, her voice barely above a whisper. "Elias... I'm not sure I'm ready." His expression softened, and he cupped her face gently, his thumb brushing against her cheek. "I can wait," he whispered, his lips inches from hers. "As long as it takes." Marisa's defenses crumbled, and when his lips met hers, she melted into him. But even in his arms, she couldn't escape the truth. There was a part of her that Elias would never know—a part that was bound to the chair and the worlds she had created. And no matter how perfect things seemed with him... Secrets had a way of unraveling everything.

7

The Ink-Stained Suit

E lias had insisted on driving her home after their night out, his charm making it impossible for Marisa to refuse. They had spent hours at an upscale rooftop restaurant, sipping wine and exchanging stories under the stars. As they pulled up in front of her building, he had flashed that irresistible smile. "Mind if I come in for a nightcap?" Marisa had hesitated, but the warmth in his eyes made her nod. Just one drink, she told herself, not realizing how much more the night would hold. The night felt different. The air in Marisa's apartment was warmer, thicker, as if the walls themselves held their breath. The soft glow of candlelight bathed the room, dancing across the shelves that lined her home library. She hadn't planned on inviting Elias over. But after their dinner—an intimate affair at a private rooftop restaurant where Elias had charmed her with stories about his global ventures—

Marisa had felt the pull. Just one more drink, she had told herself when he suggested coming back to her place. But one drink turned into two, and two turned into a bottle of deep red wine that now sat half-empty on her coffee table. Marisa laughed softly as Elias brushed a stray lock of hair from her face, his touch sending a shiver down her spine. He was perfect. His charm, his confidence—everything about him felt like a dream she hadn't realized she was longing for. But dreams were dangerous. Her mind drifted to the chair, tucked away in the corner of her library. The chair that had the power to bring stories to life. She had never told Elias about it. How could she? The chair was her secret, her burden—a power she had come to fear more than she had ever imagined.

Elias's voice was soft, his eyes studying her as he leaned back against the couch, his sleeves rolled up, exposing strong forearms that had traced over her skin just moments ago. Marisa smiled, but it didn't reach her eyes. "Just... thinking about how nice this is."

His gaze lingered on her, as if he could sense the hesitation behind her words. "You're holding back," he said, his tone gentle but probing. He's too close. Marisa stood, her pulse accelerating. "I need to freshen up. I'll be right back." She paused for a moment, her gaze lingering on Elias as a flicker of hesitation crossed her face. "Feel free to look around," she said softly, her tone casual but firm. "But..." her voice dropped, her eyes narrowing slightly, "the chair and the table in the library... they're off limits." Elias raised an eyebrow, "Off limits?" Marisa's smile was tight, her heart pounding harder. "Just... trust me, okay?" "Okay," he said softly, but his eyes wandered toward the library, the unspoken question lingering in the air. Elias nodded, his eyes following her as she disappeared down the hallway toward the bathroom.

As soon as Marisa was out of sight, Elias's eyes drifted back toward the library. She had mentioned her collection of rare books before, but he had never been inside. The room was always closed when he visited. Tonight, however, the door was slightly ajar, the glow of the lamp within casting an inviting light. She told me everything else is fair game. Elias stood, his curiosity getting the better of him. He pushed the door open and stepped inside. The library was breathtaking—floor-to-ceiling shelves filled with leather-bound classics, modern bestsellers, and everything in between. But it was the chair that caught his eye. The antique chair. It was unlike anything else in the room. The worn leather gleamed softly in the low light, and the intricate carvings along its wooden frame gave it an air of mystery.

Beside it, the small wooden table was equally worn, its surface etched with faint, almost imperceptible scratches.

Elias's brow furrowed. Why would she tell me not to touch this? He stepped closer, his fingers brushing the edge of the table. Take me home. The words, faintly etched into the wood, barely caught the light. A chill crawled up his spine. "Just a chair," he mumbled under his breath, but something about it called to him.

Elias's gaze drifted to the tall bookshelf beside the chair. His eyes landed on an old, worn copy of a slasher novel—a guilty pleasure he hadn't indulged in for years. Why not? He climbed the ladder, the wine making his movements a little too confident, a little too careless. His fingers brushed against the spine of the novel, and as he pulled it free, he lost his balance. The fall was sudden. Elias's foot slipped, and in an instant, he was tumbling backward. He hit the floor hard, a sharp pain shooting through his ankle. Groaning, he tried to push himself up, but the pain was too much. His eyes landed on the chair. Crawling, he dragged himself toward the chair, pulling the slasher novel with him. His heart pounded as he eased himself into the seat, the cool leather pressing against his back. He opened the book and began to read.

The air shifted. Elias didn't notice it at first. The

words on the page pulled him in, painting vivid images of a deranged killer stalking his victims through shadowed alleyways. The details were gruesome, the tension unmistakable. A distant noise echoed through the room—a soft creak, like a door opening. Elias's eyes flickered up, but the library was silent. His gaze returned to the book. But the room felt... different. The air was colder now, the warmth of the candles seemingly snuffed out. A chill crawled along the back of his neck, and the hair on his arms stood on end. Footsteps. Faint, almost imperceptible, but growing louder. "Marisa?" Elias's voice was barely above a whisper. No response.

A shadow moved in his peripheral vision. Elias's breath caught in his throat as his eyes darted around the room. But he was alone. Wasn't he? He turned back to the book, his hands trembling as he flipped the page. But the words seemed... different. Darker. Elias's blood ran cold. The sound of heavy breathing echoed in the silence, coming from behind him. "Run." Elias spun around, but the room was empty. But it wasn't. A shadow shifted in the corner, impossibly tall and awkwardly still. Elias's pulse skyrocketed as the figure took a step forward, the soft thud of its boots echoing through the silence. His mind screamed at him to move, to run—but his body was frozen. The story was coming to life. "Marisa..." his voice barely escaped his lips.

Marisa returned to the living room, her mind spinning with thoughts of Elias and the growing feelings she was too afraid to acknowledge. But something felt... wrong. The apartment was too quiet. "Elias?" she called, her voice echoing off the walls. Silence. Her pulse running 5 miles a minute. She moved toward the library, her heart pounding with every step. The moment she stepped inside, her breath caught in her throat. Elias was in the chair. The slasher novel lay open on his lap, and his face was pale, his throat slit, and his eyes wide with terror as he stared at something Marisa couldn't see. "Elias!" She rushed toward him Marisa's pulse pounded as she shook him, her voice trembling. "Elias, wake up!" His body was still, his eyes lifeless, and the horror of what had happened washed over her. But unlike before, Marisa didn't get pulled into the world of the book. She remained in her reality, standing there with Elias's lifeless body in the chair, the smell of blood thick in the air. The chair had finally claimed a victim.

8

Silence in the Boardroom

Marisa stood frozen; her eyes locked on Elias's lifeless body. His throat was slit, a gaping wound that painted his shirt crimson. His face, once so full of warmth and life, was now frozen in terror. His wide, unseeing eyes stared at something that wasn't there. A cold numbness washed over her, her mind refusing to process what her eyes saw. This can't be happening. Her knees buckled, and she collapsed beside him, her trembling hands reaching for his wrist. No pulse. Her fingers brushed against the still-warm skin of his neck, but the life was gone. "Elias..." her voice was barely above a whisper, cracking as tears welled in her eyes. Marisa's chest tightened, her breaths coming in short, ragged gasps. Her mind screamed at her to do something—anything—but she couldn't move. Her body was paralyzed by fear, her mind spinning in a thousand directions. This is real.

Her gaze fell to the book still open on his lap, the pages stained with blood. The Slasher. The story she had read months ago, one she had barely been able to finish because of its gruesome, relentless violence. And now, that violence had spilled into her world. "No..." Her hands shook as she touched the edge of the book, her breath catching in her throat. The chair did this. She had warned Elias. She had told him not to touch it, but curiosity—his damn curiosity—had pulled him toward it. Tears streamed down her face as the weight of what had happened crushed her. She had let him into her life. She had let him get too close. And now...He was dead because of her.

Minutes passed. Or was it hours? Marisa wasn't sure. Time had lost all meaning as she knelt beside Elias's lifeless body, her mind cycling between disbelief and raw, unrelenting terror. What do I do? The rational part of her brain—the one that hadn't been swallowed by panic—knew the truth. She couldn't call the police. How could she possibly explain this? "He sat in the chair, read a book, and the story came to life." They would think she was insane. Her stomach twisted violently, and for a moment, she thought she might be sick. But there was no time for that. Think. Marisa's gaze darted around the room, her mind racing. Cover it up. The thought slammed into her like a freight train, and for a moment, she withdrew from it. No. I can't. But what other choice did she have? If anyone found Elias here, in her home, dead... she would never be able to explain it. And if they investigated...They might discover the chair. Marisa's heart pounded louder. No one can know.

Her hands moved before her mind caught up, wiping away the tears that blurred her vision. Focus. She grabbed a towel from the nearby table and pressed it against Elias's wound, trying to stop the blood that had already long since stopped flowing. It was a useless gesture, but her hands wouldn't stop shaking.

"Clean the scene."

Marisa's movements became mechanical as she worked to erase any trace of Elias's presence in her apartment. She wiped down surfaces, removing fingerprints. She carefully collected the wine glasses they had used, washing them thoroughly before placing them back in the cabinet. Her eyes darted back to the chair, a shiver running down her spine. It looks innocent. The worn leather, the intricate carvings—but it was anything but. She approached the chair, her fingers grazing the edges of the table beside it. Take me home. The words were still faintly visible, carved into the wood like a warning she had ignored.

"How many more lives would it take?"

Her stomach twisted, but she pushed the thought

aside.

"Focus."

Marisa stared at Elias's body, her mind screaming that this was impossible, that there was no way she could do what she was about to do. But she had no choice.

"Get rid of him."

Her hands trembled as she wrapped Elias's lifeless form in a thick, heavy blanket. She struggled to lift him, her muscles screaming in protest, but adrenaline fueled her movements. Just get through this. She dragged his body out the back door, her heart pounding so loudly she was certain the neighbors would hear it. The night air was cold, biting against her skin as she struggled to move him toward her car.

"Think."

Her mind raced. Where can I take him? The woods. No one would look there. She drove in silence, her knuckles white as she gripped the steering wheel. Her breaths came in ragged gasps, her vision blurred by tears. Every bump in the road made her stomach churn. By the time she reached the remote wooded area, her body was trembling from exhaustion. She dragged Elias's body from the trunk, her muscles burning as she fought to move him deeper into the shadows. I'm sorry, Elias... Her voice was barely a whisper as she covered him, the dirt and leaves swallowing any trace of what had happened. When it was done, Marisa stood in the darkness, her body shaking, her soul feeling heavier than it ever had before.

Marisa knew she couldn't leave any loose ends. Be smart. Be thorough. She returned home and scrubbed every inch of the apartment. She removed all traces of Elias—his jacket, his phone, anything that could link him to her. The wine glasses, the blood... She crafted her alibi with meticulous care. She texted Elias's phone, sending herself a message that would make it seem as though he had gone home after their night out. She even left a voicemail. "Had a great time tonight. Call me when you get home."

"Make them think he left."

Marisa double-checked everything, her mind running through each detail over and over, making sure nothing could be traced back to her. But even as she covered her tracks, she couldn't shake the feeling that this wasn't over.

By the time Marisa finally sat down, her body was numb, her mind reeling from everything that had happened. But the weight in her chest was unbearable. Elias was gone. She had covered it up. Cleaned the scene. Created an alibi. But none of that erased the truth. The chair had taken a life. Marisa's hands trembled as she touched the edge of the table, her fingertips brushing over the carved words. Take me home. Her vision blurred with tears. How much more would the chair take before it was done with her?

9

Panic & Cover-Up

Marisa hadn't slept. The first rays of dawn filtered through her curtains, painting the room in muted shades of gold, but Marisa barely noticed. She sat curled on the edge of her bed, her arms wrapped tightly around her knees, her mind racing with thoughts she couldn't silence. Elias was gone. But his absence felt louder than his presence ever had. Every time she closed her eyes, she saw him. His lifeless body. The blood. The terror etched into his features. His unseeing eyes staring back at her. The images wouldn't leave her mind, no matter how hard she tried to push them away.

Her apartment was silent, but it felt suffocating. The air was thick, heavy with the weight of what she had done. You got rid of everything. No one will know. Marisa repeated the words in her mind like a mantra, but they offered no comfort. No matter how thoroughly she had scrubbed the floors, how carefully she had erased every trace of Elias's presence, there was a part of her that screamed you missed something. Her eyes darted around the room, paranoia clawing at her senses. What if I missed something?

Marisa had checked the apartment a dozen times—no, more than that. She had wiped down every surface, vacuumed every carpet, and inspected every inch of her home with the precision of a crime scene investigator. But it wasn't enough.

"Check again."

She pushed herself off the bed and padded into the library. Her gaze swept over the space where Elias had sat. The chair looked innocent—an antique relic that had been in the corner of her library for months. But Marisa knew better. She knelt down, her fingers grazing the floorboards where the blood had pooled. She had scrubbed until her hands were raw, but she still saw the stain, invisible to anyone but her.

"It's gone. You cleaned it."

Marisa ran her fingers along the edge of the table beside the chair, were the words "Take me home" were carved into the wood. She felt the grooves beneath her fingertips, a chilling reminder of the power the chair held. What if they find something? What if I missed a spot? Her mind conjured images of detectives combing through her apartment, finding traces of blood she had missed, matching it to Elias. She could see them standing at her door, handcuffs in hand. No. No one can know.

Marisa had always been good at disappearing. After her initial success as a bestselling author, she had retreated from the public eye, finding solace in her quiet, secluded life. But this... this was different. She wasn't just disappearing now. She was hiding. Her phone buzzed on the counter, breaking the silence.

"It's Emily."

Marisa stared at the screen, her thumb hovering over the decline button. Emily had called five times in the past two days, leaving voicemails that grew more concerned with each missed call. "Marisa, are you okay? I'm worried about you." "Please call me back. I'm starting to freak out." "Marisa, if I don't hear from you soon, I'm coming over." Her throat tightened as she listened to the messages, her fingers trembling. She deleted the voicemails, her stomach twisting with guilt. Emily wouldn't understand. She couldn't. No one can know. She ignored Daniel's texts too. He had reached out a few times, asking how she was. His words were polite, but Marisa sensed an undertone of prying. Had he heard something? Did he suspect? Paranoia gripped her mind like a vise, making it hard to breathe.

Marisa had been so meticulous. She had planned

every detail, covered her tracks, erased every trace of Elias's presence. But had she? The doubt gnawed at her. She retraced her steps over and over again, mentally replaying every moment from that night. Each thought sent a fresh wave of panic crashing over her. Her mind spiraled as she imagined the tiniest of mistakes leading to her downfall. All it takes is one slip. One small mistake.

Days passed. Marisa barely left her apartment. She avoided her neighbors, kept the curtains drawn, and ignored every phone call. Her world had shrunk to the confines of her home—a prison she had built for herself. Her paranoia grew with each passing hour. Every noise outside her door made her heart stop. The sound of footsteps in the hallway sent her mind spiraling with worst-case scenarios.

"They're coming. They know."

Her nights were worse. The silence was suffocating, her mind refusing to let her rest. Elias's eyes haunted her. She tried to distract herself with books, but every story felt hollow, lifeless. None of them could compare to the realities she had lived through the chair. But the chair was silent now. It sat in the corner of her library, an ominous presence that she refused to look at. She couldn't go near it. Not after what had happened. But what if I need it? The thought ran circles around her mind, uninvited and unwelcome. What if the chair could fix this? Marisa shook her head, her jaw clenched. No. She had sworn she would never use it again. But what if— "No." Her voice was barely a whisper, but it echoed through the empty room. The chair was too dangerous. But as the days stretched on, the weight of her paranoia and guilt grew heavier. And deep down, Marisa knew... It was only a matter of time before she broke.

10

Becoming a Suspect

M arisa had been avoiding the outside world for days, but she couldn't avoid this. The knock on her door was firm—three solid taps that echoed through her apartment, making her heart leap into her throat. She froze, her body stiffening as the echoes faded.

"Calm down. It's probably nothing."

But deep down, she knew better. Her hands trembled as she wiped them on her jeans, forcing her feet to move toward the door. When she opened it, her breath trapped in her throat. Detective Michael Bennett. He stood there, tall and imposing, with sharp intense eyes that missed nothing. His suit was immaculate, his tie perfectly knotted. But it was the intensity in his gaze that sent a chill down Marisa's spine. "Miss Cole?" His voice was calm, but there was a weight behind it that made her skin crawl. "Y-

Yes?" Marisa's voice barely managed to escape her lips. "I'm Detective Bennett. I'd like to ask you a few questions about Elias Kingston." Her stomach dropped as if she had been on a roller coaster.

"Stay calm. You've prepared for this."

"Of course," she said, her voice steadier than she felt. She stepped aside, allowing him to enter.

The living room felt suffocating with Bennett in it. Marisa's pulse pounded in her ears as she gestured toward the couch. "Would you like something to drink?" she asked, her voice a touch too high, too eager. "No, thank you." Bennett's polite smile didn't reach his eyes. He pulled out a small notebook and a pen, sitting down with practiced ease. "This won't take long." Marisa perched on the edge of the chair across from him, her hands clasped tightly in her lap. "When was the last time you saw Mr. Kingston?" Marisa swallowed hard.

"Stick to the story."

"Um... after dinner some nights ago." Her voice felt distant, as if she were hearing herself speak from underwater. "We had a nice evening. He dropped me off, and... that was the last time I saw him." "Is something wrong?" Bennett's pen moved across the page, his expression unreadable. "Did he mention where he was going afterward?" Marisa shook her head, her throat dry. "No. He just... said he'd call me later." "Did he?" Her heart pounded harder.

Lie.!

"No," she whispered. "He didn't." Bennett's eyes lifted, locking onto hers.

"He's studying you."

"Strange," he whispered, tapping his pen against the notebook. "His car was found abandoned about two miles from here." Marisa's blood turned to ice. "Abandoned?" "Yes. No signs of forced entry, no struggle." Bennett's gaze never hesitated. "You said he dropped you off. Did you notice anything unusual about him that night?" Marisa shook her head quickly, her palms damp with sweat. "No. He seemed... fine."

"LIAR."

Bennett's silence stretched on, the weight of it pressing down on her. "Miss Cole," he said softly, but there was an edge to his tone that made her heart race. "If there's anything—anything at all— that you remember, now's the time to tell me." "I told you everything," Marisa whispered, her voice barely above a breath. Bennett's eyes lingered on her for a moment too long before he nodded, closing his notebook. But the look in his eyes told her he didn't believe her.

After the detective left, Marisa barely had time to catch her breath before her phone buzzed. Emily was calling again. Marisa hesitated, her thumb hovering over the screen. Ignore it. But guilt gnawed at her insides. She couldn't ignore Emily forever. "Hey," Marisa, forcing her voice to sound normal. "Marisa." Emily's voice was softer than usual, but there was a tightness beneath it. "Are you okay?" Marisa's stomach twisted. "I'm fine. Just... tired." There was a long pause. "Are you sure?" Emily asked carefully. "I heard about Elias." "They say he just vanished."

Marisa's throat went dry. Of course she heard. "Yeah... it's terrible," Marisa said, her voice barely above a whisper. Emily's silence was heavy. "When was the last time you saw him?" Marisa's heart skipped a beat. "After dinner that night," she lied. "Why?" "Because..." Emily's voice trailed off, her hesitation sending a chill down Marisa's spine. "Something doesn't feel right, Marisa." "I mean... you've been different lately. Distant. And now Elias is missing..." Marisa's grip on the phone tightened. "Emily, I'm fine." "Are you?" Emily's voice was filled with concern, but there was something else beneath it now. Marisa's armpits become sweaty. "Emily, please... just drop it." But Emily's silence told Marisa that her friend wasn't going to let this go.

Days passed, but the tension only grew. Detective Bennett stopped by again, each visit more intense than the last. He asked the same questions, but in different ways—testing her. Marisa's lies felt thinner with each passing day, and Bennett could sense it. And then there was Emily. Emily wasn't just concerned anymore. She was suspicious. Marisa caught her friend glancing around her apartment during her last visit, her eyes lingering on the library door for too long.

"You've been spending a lot of time alone," Emily had said softly, her gaze searching Marisa's face. "I just needed space," Marisa said, but Emily's eyes told her she didn't believe that. And then, Emily started asking questions about the past—about Marisa's writing, her sudden withdrawal from the world. She's digging. Marisa's mind raced. Emily knows something. And if she kept digging... She would find out.

Marisa couldn't keep up the act forever. The pressure was suffocating, the walls closing in on her from every direction. She barely slept. Her mind was constantly racing, searching for any cracks in her story, any tiny detail that could unravel everything. One mistake. That's all it would take. Emily's texts grew more frequent. Bennett's questions grew sharper. Marisa could feel their suspicion circling her like vultures. They're too close. She had done everything right. Hadn't she? But now... now it felt like everything was unraveling. And Marisa knew that if they kept digging, if they found the truth about what had happened to Elias... It would destroy her.

11

A Dangerous Read

Marisa stood in front of the chair, her breath shallow and tight. The room was still, crowded with silence, the only sound the faint hum of the heater and the steady thump of her pulse in her ears. Her fingers reached out, almost of their own accord, grazing the edge of the table beside it— tracing the old, worn carvings she'd come to know all too well. Her fingertips hovered over the etched words as if they might burn her. *Take me home.* The phrase was simple. Innocent, even. But not to her. Not anymore. It stared back at her now like a secret scrawled in plain sight, a phrase soaked in memory and consequence. The words were a doorway. A contract. A key to something beyond the reach of logic. They were a whisper of escape when the world closed in. But now... escape wasn't enough.

Now, that power wasn't just about wonder or

exploration. It wasn't about curiosity or control. It was about *survival*. The last few days played on repeat in her mind, each moment stitched together by growing fear. Detective Bennett's voice—too calm, too precise—still rang in her ears. His questions had shifted lately, becoming tighter, more focused. He was digging. Patient, methodical. Dangerous.

And then there was Emily. Sweet, loyal Emily. The one person Marisa hadn't wanted to lose. But her eyes had changed—lingering longer when Marisa spoke, narrowing when she thought Marisa wasn't looking. Her voice had softened too much, careful in a way that screamed suspicion. *"You've been different lately, Marisa." "It's like you're not really here anymore "What's going on?"* They were both closing in. They would find out. They would unravel everything she had so carefully hidden, so desperately built. And if they did—if they discovered the truth about the chair, the stories, the consequences—her life wouldn't just fall apart. It would *end*.

Not in a literal sense, maybe. But whatever pieces of herself she still had left—whatever fragile grip she had on this version of her life—they would vanish. She looked down at the chair. Quiet. But the power pulsing beneath its surface was undeniable. Once, it had given her freedom. Now, it might be the only thing that could save her. Her hands curled into fists at her sides. Her decision wasn't made yet, but the moment was close. She could feel it rising, like a wave she could no longer hold back. Because running out of time meant one thing: She might need to write her way out again. And this time, someone else might not come back.

"Don't let that happen."

Marisa's eyes darkened as a new thought took root, twisting its way through her mind. The chair. It had taken Elias. It had the power to take others too. No one would ever know. The idea horrified her. But as much as she tried to push it away, it lingered, whispering promises of safety. One more story. One more sacrifice. And everything would be fine.

Marisa sat down at her desk, her pulse thrumming loud and uneven in her ears like the ticking of a countdown clock. The glow of her laptop screen cast a pale wash across her face, the rest of the room cloaked in shadows. Her fingers hovered above the keyboard, trembling ever so slightly as she opened a blank document. *"Just a story,"* she whispered, the words barely audible, more breath than sound. She clung to the lie like a life raft, trying to convince herself that what she was about to do didn't matter. That this was fiction—no more real than the characters she had dreamed up before. Another narrative. Another escape. But she knew better.

The chair had shown her the truth. Stories *lived*.

Words had weight now. And this one would bleed. Her hands moved with a sudden, unnatural steadiness, guided by something deeper than thought. The keys clicked rapidly under her fingers as scenes formed in her mind—twisted, sharp, and deliberate. She spun her tale with the precision of a blade. *Stories that would kill.* She paused only once—when she typed the title: *Emily's Misfortune.* A tightness gripped her soul. Emily. Her best friend. The one person who had stood by her when the world fell apart. The one who had shown up with soup, with sarcasm, with truth. Who had cared when no one else had.

But Emily had crossed a line. She was asking too many questions. Digging where she shouldn't. And in this story, curiosity came with consequences. Marisa stared at the screen, her jaw clenched. Her hands trembled again, not from fear—but from the weight of what she was becoming. Because this wasn't just a story. This was a warning. Or maybe... a sentence.

Asking questions. Getting too close. Marisa's fingers trembled as she crafted the narrative—a tragic story where Emily, in her curiosity, stumbled upon a truth that led her into danger. A hit- and-run, an unfortunate accident that would never be traced back to Marisa. Her vision blurred as her emotions warred with her actions, but her fingers didn't stop typing. "I'm sorry, Emily."

Marisa barely had time to catch her breath before she opened another document. "The Detective's Last Case." Bennett was sharp—too sharp. His persistence was like a shadow that followed her, always one step behind. Marisa could feel him closing in. If he found out... Her mind spun a chilling tale where Bennett, relentless in his pursuit of justice, uncovered secrets he wasn't supposed to know. His obsession led him to an untimely end—a violent confrontation with a dangerous criminal, a staged event that would leave no trace of Marisa's involvement. Her hands shook as she wrote, her breaths coming in shallow gasps. This wasn't who she was. But it was who she needed to be. To survive.

The stories were finished. Perfect. Flawless. Deadly. Each word had been chosen with precision, each sentence carefully laced with purpose. They weren't just narratives anymore—they were weapons. Traps dressed as fiction. Now, all that remained was to get them read. In the chair. Where the stories would no longer stay on the page. Marisa's mind buzzed, both electric and cold, as she refined her plan. Emily would be the easy one. All it would take was warmth—something familiar. A simple coffee date, an innocent conversation over lattes and laughter. She'd plant the seed gently, like she always had. *"I've been working on something new,"* she'd said, her voice light and casual. *"A mystery. Dark, twisty. I think you'll love it."*

Emily never said no. She cared too much. Trusted too easily. This time, the setting had to be just right. Controlled. *"I've been working from home a lot lately,"* Marisa said over the phone, letting the words flow naturally, like small talk. *"Come by. Read it here while I make us some tea. I'd love to see your reaction in real time."* Emily agreed without hesitation. Of course she did. Marisa smiled to herself as she hung up the call, her fingers brushing the edge of the chair. The trap was set. But Bennett... Bennett would be harder.

He was sharp—too sharp. He read between the lines. Saw things most people missed. He was already suspicious, already watching her more closely than she liked. Bringing him here would take more than charm. It would take strategy. Patience. A misstep with him could unravel everything. Marisa leaned back in the chair, her eyes narrowing. She wasn't worried—yet. But she knew that getting Bennett into the seat would require more than an invitation. It would require precision. And maybe... persuasion. After all, everyone had a weakness. She just had to find his.

Marisa needed a different approach. An anonymous tip. A carefully placed envelope with a letter left at the precinct, addressed to him. A story he wouldn't be able to resist. But this time, her plan had an extra layer. The letter would contain just enough information about Elias's disappearance— just enough to pique Bennett's interest and make him want to question her. "You're too curious, Detective." Marisa's lips curled into a grim smile. She knew Bennett. Once he took the bait, he wouldn't be able to resist confronting her. Bennett would come. They both would. And when they did... They would sit in the chair. They would read. And they would never leave the same. They would never see it coming.

The envelope sat alone on the front steps of the Cedar Hollow Police Precinct, resting neatly on the top stair like it had been *placed* there—deliberate, silent, waiting to be found. The pale manila surface stood out against the chipped gray concrete, impossibly clean in a town where dust settled fast and unnoticed things were usually left to rot. Detective Bennett spotted it the moment he stepped outside for air. The late afternoon sun hung low, casting long shadows across the sidewalk and turning the precinct's windows into mirrors. The stillness was unsettling—the kind that comes right before a storm. No wind. No passing cars. Just the envelope.

He frowned and moved toward it, the crunch of gravel beneath his boots loud in the otherwise silent parking lot. His instincts prickled as he knelt to pick it up. No return address. No postage. Just his name, written in clean, even handwriting across the front: *Detective M. Bennett.* His fingers hovered for a second before he picked it up. The paper was cool to the touch. He flipped it over. Sealed. Untouched. No markings. No fingerprints—at least none he could see. But everything about it screamed *intentional*. Someone had been here. Recently. And they knew exactly where to leave it.

He glanced toward the building behind him—the worn brick facade of Cedar Hollow's modest precinct, more government leftovers than fortress. Inside, everything was routine: old desks, worn chairs, a coffeepot that hadn't been cleaned in weeks. Outside, the air felt different. *Watched.* Bennett straightened slowly, eyes sweeping the street. It was empty. Too empty. And in Cedar Hollow, that was never a good sign. He slipped the envelope into the inside pocket of his coat, heart ticking a little faster. Someone wanted him to see this. To follow something. And the game had just begun.

12

A Door That Wouldn't Open

M arisa had been so sure her plan would work. Everything was perfect. The stories were crafted with deadly precision. "Emily's Misfortune" was a tragic tale of a woman who stumbled upon a dark truth and met an untimely end. "The Detective's Last Case" was a gritty, unsettling narrative of a relentless cop who got too close to a dangerous secret—one that cost him his life. All they had to do was read them. In the chair. And everything would be fine. But plans, no matter how carefully designed, had a way of unraveling.

Marisa had been meticulous in planning how to get Emily to read the story in the chair. "Come by for coffee, Emily. I want your thoughts on the manuscript, I finally finished it." Emily, ever the supportive friend, hadn't hesitated. She never did. That was what Marisa was counting on. The manuscript sat innocently on the antique table. The chair—the gateway—was waiting, its presence a silent predator in the corner of her home library. Marisa had guided Emily toward it with practiced ease, her voice light, her movements casual. "It's just a rough draft," Marisa had said, her heart pounding beneath her calm exterior. "But I'd love your thoughts before I send it out." Emily smiled, her guard lowered, and sat down. In the chair. Yes.

Marisa's breath caught as Emily picked up the manuscript and began to read. The story was unfolding. But then... Emily's expression changed. Her eyes narrowed, her smile faded, and a shadow of doubt crossed her face. "What is this, Marisa?" Emily's voice was softer now, but there was an edge—a hesitation that sent chills down Marisa's spine. "Just something I've been working on," Marisa replied, her throat dry. "A mystery. I thought you'd enjoy it." Emily's fingers moved slowly across the pages, her brow furrowed in quiet concentration. Then— hesitation. She tilted her head slightly, her lips parting in uncertainty. "It feels... weird," Emily says, barely above a whisper. Marisa stiffened, watching every twitch of Emily's expression. The words hung in the air like static.

Emily's gaze drifted toward the chair. Her body shifted—just a subtle inch backward, but enough. Enough to show discomfort. Mistrust. A sense that

71

something was *off*. "I'm not really feeling this right now," she added, standing abruptly. "Mind if I take it home and read it later?" Marisa's stomach plummeted. A cold wave of panic swept over her, her breath catching before she could respond. "Oh, sure," she said quickly—*too* quickly—her voice brittle and falsely bright, like cracked glass barely holding together. She tried to mask the rising dread with a smile, but it didn't reach her eyes. She sat frozen, helpless, as Emily placed the manuscript gently back on the table and rose to her feet—completely untouched by the chair's magic. No shift. No change. No ripple of entry.

The plan had failed. Marisa's eyes locked on Emily, searching for a sign—*anything*—that something had happened. But there was nothing. Just warmth. Familiarity. A dangerous calm. Then Emily glanced at the chair again. Just for a moment. But it was *too* long. Her gaze lingered like a question she hadn't asked out loud. "I'll text you after I read it, okay?" Emily said. Her voice was light, friendly—*but distant*. There was something in it that hadn't been there before. Doubt. Suspicion.

Marisa forced a smile. Her hands clenched into fists, nails digging into her palms. "Yeah. Sure. Take your time." She watched as Emily stepped through the doorway and disappeared down the hall. The door clicked shut. And in the silence that followed,

Marisa felt it. The first crack of dread, sharp and cold, splintering through her whole body. The chair hadn't worked. Emily was still herself. And now... she was walking away with the story. And Marisa didn't know if she'd be coming back.

Bennett was supposed to be easier. Predictable. Methodical. A man ruled by curiosity and procedure. Marisa had played him like a piano—each note struck with precision. The anonymous tip had been crafted perfectly: a carefully layered lie about Elias Kingston's death, just plausible enough to raise alarms, just murky enough to lure a detective into chasing shadows. She knew Bennett couldn't resist a breadcrumb trail, especially when it threatened to lead to the truth. What she hadn't expected... was how quickly he'd show up. The knock at her door that evening was like a gunshot through her stomach. Marisa froze, every nerve on high alert. For a split second, she debated pretending not to be home. But then she caught her reflection—pale, tight-lipped, eyes wide—and she forced it away. She swallowed hard and opened the door. There he stood.

Detective Bennett. Tall, composed, every inch of him wrapped in calm authority. But it was his eyes that made her stomach lurch—those calculating, unblinking eyes that never missed anything. "Detective Bennett," she said sweetly, pulling a mask of innocence over the panic rising in her throat. She summoned a smile, soft and effortless, but her pulse thundered behind her ribs. "What brings you here?" "I got an interesting piece of information about Elias Kingston," he said evenly. His voice was smooth— too smooth. Neutral on the surface, but beneath it, a current of suspicion. He scanned her face, quiet and unblinking. But his eyes—his eyes *burned*. Sharp. Dissecting.

Marisa's blood ran cold. *He doesn't know. He can't know. He doesn't know I sent it.* She kept her smile, let it stretch just a bit wider, feigning curiosity. "Oh?" she asked, voice just above a whisper. "That sounds serious." "May I come in?" he said. She hesitated for a beat too long. Then stepped aside. "Of course," she said, smoothing her tone into something welcoming. As he crossed the threshold, her mind ignited. Every thought fired at once. Every step he took into her space felt like a countdown. She had to stay calm. She had to stay in control. This was it. The trap was set. But now, she was standing inside it too. And Bennett? He was already looking for the cracks.

As they stood in her library, Marisa carefully guided the conversation, keeping her tone relaxed, her smile easy.

"Now. Bring up the manuscript. Make it sound natural."

"You know, I've been working on something," she said, her voice perfectly casual. "A manuscript. It's about a detective. Thought maybe you could give me some pointers?" Bennett's eyebrow lifted. "A detective?" "What kind of case?" Marisa reached for the manuscript, her fingers brushing lightly against the worn pages. She placed it gently on the antique table beside the chair. All he had to do was sit. "It's gritty," she murmured, her pulse pounding. "But I'd love your feedback." Bennett glanced at the manuscript, then—to Marisa's dismay—he didn't sit. "I'll take it with me," he said casually "I'll read it later."

"No. No, no, no."

Marisa's throat tightened. "Oh... I was hoping you'd read a little now. Just to tell me if it's realistic." Her voice was calm, but her palms were sweating. Bennett's gaze sharpened. Something in his eyes shifted. "Maybe later," he said, his tone polite but distant. Guarded. Why won't you sit?

Marisa watched him leave, the manuscript tucked under his arm. Untouched by the chair. Two failed attempts. She stood in the middle of her living room, her mind spiraling. It should have worked. Her plans had been flawless. Why hadn't it worked?

The plan had been perfect. Why did they resist? Her thoughts spiraled, her mind racing with possibilities. Did they suspect something? Did they know? Emily's hesitation. Bennett's refusal. They felt it. They sensed something was wrong. I was so close. Her mind screamed at her to stop—to burn the stories, to destroy the chair, to walk away. But she was too far gone.

13

Truth on Her Trail

D etective Michael Bennett was a man who trusted his gut. And his gut was screaming at him now. Sitting in his dimly lit office, Bennett stared at the whiteboard plastered with notes, timelines, and photos from Elias Kingston's disappearance. Red strings connected people, locations, and evidence, but the pattern that should have formed wasn't there. Something didn't fit. "Why would she lie about the smallest details?" Bennett muttered to himself, running a hand through his graying hair. His jaw clenched as he reviewed the timeline again. Marisa Cole. The once-famous author who had retreated from the public eye. Her name was all over this case, yet her version of events had subtle gaps. Her timeline after the dinner with Elias was too clean. Too perfect.

Bennett had been a cop long enough to know

that when stories were too neat, they were usually false. "What are you hiding, Marisa?" he whispered, narrowing his eyes as he flipped through the restaurant surveillance footage from the night Elias disappeared.

The first time Bennett visited Marisa's apartment, she had been charming, polite, and disarmingly composed. But that had been four visits ago. Now, things were different. Bennett stood at her door again, his eyes scanning the surroundings before he knocked. This time, he wasn't leaving without answers. Marisa opened the door, her smile strained. Her eyes, which once held quiet confidence, were now shadowed with exhaustion. "Detective," she greeted, her voice just a touch too cheerful. "Ms. Cole," Bennett replied, stepping inside without waiting for an invitation. Marisa's apartment was immaculate—too immaculate. Every surface was spotless, every object in its place. But Bennett noticed the slight tremor in her hands as she gestured for him to sit. "Coffee?" she offered, her tone light, but Bennett could see the tension in her shoulders. "No, thank you." He sat down, his eyes never leaving hers. "I just have a few more questions."

Marisa's smile faltered. "Again?" "Just clarifying a few things." Bennett leaned forward, his eyes narrowing slightly. "What did you do after Elias dropped you off?" Marisa blinked. Too long. "I went

straight to sleep. It was a long day. I told you that."
Bennett with his intense stare. "And you didn't leave
again?" "No. Why would I?" Her voice was steady,
but Bennett saw the trace of anxiety in her eyes. "You
sure?" A bead of sweat formed at the base of her neck.
"Positive." Bennett leaned back, tapping his pen
against the notepad in his hand. "You seem... tense,
Ms. Cole." "I'm just tired, Detective." She rubbed
her temples, offering a small, strained smile. "All of
this... it's exhausting."

As soon as Bennett left, Marisa's facade crumbled.
Her hands shook as she locked the door behind him,
her heart pounding in her ears.

"He knows."

The thought echoed through her mind like a drum-
beat. He's getting too close. Marisa paced the length
of her living room, her mind racing. She replayed
every conversation she'd had with Bennett, analyz-
ing every word, every glance. "Why didn't he believe
me?" she whispered, her voice trembling. Her mind
spun with paranoia. Had she missed something? A
fingerprint? A trace of blood? No. I was careful. I
covered everything. But what if she hadn't? Her
thoughts spiraled, each one more terrifying than
the last. Had Bennett found something? Was he
just toying with her now? Waiting for her to slip?
Marisa's pulse raced as her paranoia consumed her.
He's not going to stop.

Bennett wasn't one to give up. He had been a cop for too long to ignore the feeling in his gut. "Something's off," he muttered as he replayed all the security footage again. And then... There it was. A security camera near Marisa's home. Bennett had reviewed it several times before, but now, he noticed something he had missed. Elias's car. It was parked down the street from Marisa's apartment. Two hours after Elias was supposedly gone. Bennett's jaw tightened as he leaned closer to the screen. "Why would his car still be there?" The footage didn't capture Marisa getting into the car, but its presence was damning. She lied. Bennett's eyes narrowed. "And now, I know where to push."

Bennett didn't confront Marisa immediately. He was a hunter. And she was prey. Let her think she's safe. Bennett began tightening the net around her, visiting her apartment more frequently, asking the same questions over and over. "You're sure you didn't see Elias again that night?" "Positive," Marisa would say, her smile growing thinner with each visit. "And you went straight home?" "Yes." But each time Bennett asked, Marisa's answers grew shakier. Her composure was slipping. He did this because he knew at some point she would break.

Marisa couldn't breathe. Her world was closing in. Bennett knew. He was circling closer. Every visit, every question, tightened the noose around her neck.

Her nights were restless, filled with nightmares of Bennett standing over her, demanding answers. "Tell me the truth, Marisa." His voice echoed in her mind, relentless and unforgiving. Marisa's sanity teetered on the edge. I have to stop him. Her mind screamed for a solution. Time is running out. Marisa's desperation clawed at her insides. Every second that passed brought Bennett closer to the truth.

14

Writing Her Way Out

Marisa stared at the blank page on her laptop screen, her fingers hovering over the keyboard. Her body was numb, her mind an echo chamber of fear and regret. The walls were closing in. Bennett was circling like a predator, asking the same questions over and over. Each visit felt closer, sharper. And Emily... Emily's silence was worse than anything. Marisa hadn't heard from her in days. She knows. That thought gnawed at her insides like a cancer. There was no way out. Unless... Her eyes drifted to the chair in the corner of her home library. The chair. Her pulse slowed. The escape was right there. Marisa's throat tightened as she pushed the thought away. But it was too late. It had taken root.

The idea burrowed deeper, feeding on her fear. The chair could end this. No more questions. No more fear. No more running. Her body moved on autopilot as she opened a new document. "Just one more story." Her hands trembled as she typed, each keystroke heavier than the last. "Marisa Cole sat in her favorite chair, a glass of wine in her hand. The weight of her secrets pressed down on her, but for the first time, she felt... calm. She knew what needed to be done. One final act. One final escape. And as her eyes closed, she welcomed the stillness that followed." Marisa paused, her fingers hovering over the keys. It wasn't enough. The words felt... hollow. Too clinical. "No." If this was her last story, it had to be perfect. "Make it real." Her mind painting a vivid, heartbreaking scene—one that felt more real than any story she'd ever written.

"The sun had just begun to set, casting a warm, golden glow across the room. The air was thick with the scent of jasmine, her favorite candle burning softly on the table beside her. Marisa Cole sat in her chair, a glass of deep red wine resting in her hand. The rim of the glass was smudged with her lipstick, a delicate shade of rose. She barely tasted the wine as it touched her lips. It was the ritual that mattered—the quiet act of saying goodbye. She wore her favorite sweater, the soft wool wrapping around her like a gentle embrace. Her hair was loosely tied back, a few strands falling to frame her face. The house was silent, the world outside muffled and distant. In that moment, she was alone.

Completely... finally... alone. Her eyes stuck on the bookshelves that lined her walls—stories that had been her escape for years. Worlds she had disappeared into to avoid her own. But not this time. This was her ending. Marisa's breathing slowed as she leaned back in the chair, her body sinking into the worn leather. She closed her eyes, letting the stillness wrap around her. No more running. No more fear. Just... peace. Her fingers loosened around the glass as her breathing grew shallow. Her mind drifted, her thoughts growing softer, quieter... until there was nothing but silence. Perfect silence."

The manuscript was finished. Marisa's body felt heavy as she stood, the printed pages in her hand. Her footsteps echoed as she crossed the room. The chair waited for her, its presence almost... inviting. The air was heavier near it, charged with an unseen energy that made her skin prickle. "This is the only way." Her pulse slowed as her fingertips brushed the leather. Cold. Unforgiving. Her knees felt weak as she lowered herself into the chair, her body sinking into its familiar embrace. A shiver crawled down her spine as she rested her back against the worn leather, the chair molding itself to her shape like it had been waiting for her. It was waiting.

Her hands trembled as she set the manuscript on her lap, her fingers brushing over the pages. The words she had written... her own death. The air thickened, pressing down on her chest, making it hard to breathe. "Just read it." Her voice was barely a whisper as her eyes landed on the first line. Surrendering to the words "Marisa Cole sat in her favorite chair..." Her pulse pounded in her ears like 10,000 drums, but her body felt... lighter. The world around her shifted.

The scent of jasmine filled her nostrils, stronger now—too real. The dim glow of the sunset bathed the room in a golden hue that wasn't there moments ago. Her eyes scanned the words again, her breath catching in her throat as she read. "The weight of her secrets pressed down on her, but for the first time, she felt... calm." A wave of warmth washed over her. The chair was pulling her in. As she began to read her surroundings blurred at the edges, the line between reality and fiction dissolving as the story unfolded. The glass of wine appeared in her hand—a perfect mimic of what she had described. Her lips brushed against the rim, and the cool liquid slid down her throat, just as she had written. Her own words were becoming real. Her breathing slowed as her body relaxed further. It was working.

Her vision grew hazy as the silence wrapped around her, pulling her deeper into the narrative. "No more running." Her pulse slowed, her body sinking deeper. Her eyelids fluttered as the words whispered in her mind. "No more fear." Her breathing grew shallower. "Just... peace." A calm, almost seductive warmth spread through her limbs. It felt so real. Too real.

Barely a whisper in the back of her mind. But it was enough. "No." The word echoed through her thoughts like a distant cry. Her heart slammed against her rib-cage. "This isn't right." A cold chill crept up her spine, cutting through the false warmth that had wrapped around her. "Something's wrong." Her fingers twitched, her grip on the manuscript tightening. The words blurred as her vision clouded, her mind screaming at her to stop. "I don't want this." Her pulse spiked, her body screaming in protest as the chair's pull grew stronger. "This isn't real." Her throat constricted as a surge of raw panic surged through her veins. "Get out." Her mind screamed, her body refusing to move.

The chair wasn't letting her go. Her fingers trembled as she gripped the edges of the manuscript, her vision darkening as the false peace tried to drag her deeper. "I can't..." "Take me home." The words erupted from her lips in a desperate, broken whisper. Marisa's body lurched forward as reality slammed back into her. She gasped, her lungs burning as she tore herself away from the chair. The manuscript slipped from her fingers, the pages scattering across the floor. Her body collapsed onto the ground, her chest heaving as she fought to catch her breath. She was alive. But her body trembled, her skin clammy with cold sweat. "I almost..." The words stuck in her throat. Her vision blurred as her eyes landed on the manuscript sprawled across the floor. Her death. It was too easy. Too real. The chair's power was growing. And this time... it almost won.

Marisa's body shook as she pulled her knees to her stomach, her mind still reeling. "I can't." Her voice was barely above a whisper, her throat raw from screaming. Her eyes stayed glued to the manuscript. She had written her own death. And the chair had tried to make it real. "It's stronger than I thought." Her breathing slowed as realization settled in.

15

The Final Attempt

Marisa's hands trembled as she stood in front of her desk, her eyes bloodshot and heavy with exhaustion. This was it. Her throat tightened, her body stiff with tension as she stared at the empty document on her laptop screen. Her last chance. The weight of her guilt had grown too heavy to bear. Every time she closed her eyes, she saw Elias's lifeless body sprawled on the floor. The blood. The silence. Her fault. Marisa's breath hitched. "I can't fix this." "I can fix this!"

The words echoed in her mind, a desperate mantra she clung to as she forced herself to breathe. The chair had taken him. But maybe... it could give him back. Marisa's throat burned as her eyes drifted toward the antique chair in the corner. Its presence was heavier now, suffocating the air in the room. "One more story." Her mind screamed at her to stop, to walk away. But it was too late for that. She couldn't live with this. If she didn't fix this… She wouldn't survive.

Marisa sat down, her breathing shallow as she placed her fingers on the keyboard. "Just one more." Her vision blurred as tears filled her eyes, but she forced herself to type. "The night unfolded differently this time." Her hands trembled as she painted the scene with meticulous detail. "Elias entered her home, his eyes warm and full of curiosity. But this time, Marisa was ready." Her mind conjured an alternate reality—one where she didn't fail.

"When Elias's eyes landed on the antique chair, Marisa moved quickly, her voice cutting through the quiet. 'Don't sit there,' she says, her words laced with urgency." She imagined the relief that would fill her if she could stop him. "Elias turned, his brow furrowed with confusion. 'Why?' he asked softly." "Because it's dangerous," she whispered. "Please… just trust me." Marisa fingers flew across the keyboard, crafting a moment where he listened— where he stepped away from the chair. "Elias pulled his hand back, the danger passing like a shadow.

He never touched the chair. And Marisa's night-mare… never began." Her chest tightened, the knot of guilt and fear pressing harder against her ribs. "This time, Elias lived." Marisa's hands shook vi-olently as she typed the final words. "This time, I saved him." She stared at the words on the screen, her vision blurred by tears. It was perfect. Too perfect. A hollow ache settled deep in her spirit. "Please..." Her voice was barely a whisper as she saved the document. "Let this work."

The manuscript was finish printing. Marisa's legs felt like lead as she walked toward the chair, her breathing shallow. The air grew thicker with every step, pressing down on her like an invisible weight. The chair was waiting. It knew. Her heart pushing out of her chest as she sat down, the cool leather sending a shiver through her body. This time... it's different. The chair's grip was stronger—hungrier. Marisa's hands shook as she placed the manuscript on her lap, her fingers brushing over the fresh pages. "One last time." Her throat constricted as her eyes scanned the first line. "The night unfolded differently this time..." The moment she read the words aloud, the air shifted. The world around her tilted. The scent of wine. The soft glow of the fireplace. The boundaries between fiction and reality collapsed.

Marisa's breath caught as her surroundings shifted. The familiar warmth of that night enveloped her—the night Elias died. She was back. Her stomach clenched as she saw him, alive and standing just feet away. "Elias..." Her voice was barely above a whisper, her body frozen as she watched the scene unfold before her. Everything was exactly the same.

The wine. The dim lighting. Her heart slammed against her ribs as she saw herself move through the room—guiding Elias toward the library. "Stop." Marisa's mind screamed at her to intervene. "Don't let him touch it." But her legs felt like lead, her body bound by the chair's unrelenting grip. "Move."

Her breath quickened as she fought to push forward, her body trembling as she struggled to break free. "Elias!" Her voice echoed through the room, but he didn't hear her. Her pulse hammered as she watched herself leave the room, leaving Elias alone. "No." Her throat went dry as Elias's curiosity drew him toward the bookshelf, toward the chair. "Not again." Marisa's pulse spiked as panic settled in her mind. "Please." Her voice was a desperate whisper as she watched Elias climb the ladder. "Turn around." Her throat on fire as the scene played out before her exactly as it had that night. Elias's fingers brushed against the worn leather of the chair. "STOP!" Her scream echoed, but it was too late.

Marisa's heart stopped. Elias's hand touched the chair, and everything unraveled. The chair had already claimed him. Her body felt as though it was being ripped apart. Her lungs seized as the air thickened around her, suffocating her as the scene unfolded. Elias sat down. Her stomach dropped as the chair's power surged. "NO!" Her throat burned as she screamed, her body convulsing as she fought to break free. But she couldn't stop it. Her pulse hammered, her chest jerking as the horror unfolded before her. Elias's body slumped forward, his throat slit—just like before.

The blood spilled onto the floor, painting the nightmare she had tried so desperately to erase. "No… no…" Her vision blurred as her body convulsed, the weight of her failure crushing her. "I did everything right." Her voice cracked as she watched him die again. "I fixed it…" Her body trembling as she felt the weight of the chair's power anchoring her to this moment. "Why didn't it work?" Tears streamed down her face as reality unraveled around her. The chair had never intended to let her change fate. It was always in control.

Marisa's body sagged as the weight of her failure crushed her. Her breath coming in shallow gasps as she watched the blood pool beneath Elias's body. Nothing had changed. Fate was immutable. Her pulse slowed, her body trembling as the realization hit her with brutal clarity. "The chair… lied to me." Her vision blurred as the scene faded, the familiar sensation of being ripped away from the past slamming into her.

Marisa gasped as she was hurled back into reality, her body collapsing onto the floor beside the chair. Her chest throbbed as she struggled to breathe, tears streaming down her face. "I failed." Her voice was faint as her body convulsed, wracked with sobs. Elias was gone. Her vision blurred as she stared at the manuscript on the floor. Her perfect story. And it meant nothing. The chair had never given her a choice. It had always been in control.

16

The Quiet Decision

Marisa sat motionless in the chair. The manuscript lay discarded on the floor, stained with her tears. The room was silent... but her mind was not. "You can fix this." The voice echoed softly, a cruel whisper from the corners of her fractured mind. "Just one more story." Her body trembling as she stared at the chair beneath her. The chair that had taken so much. Elias. Her sanity. Her life. Marisa's breath caught as her vision blurred, her mind spiraling between reality and the fiction she had crafted. "You don't have to stop. You don't have to feel this pain." The chair was still offering her a way out. Escape.

Her fingers curled over the armrests, her knuckles turning white as her body fought against the pull. "Just read one more story." The words slithered through her mind, seductive and familiar. "Bring him back. Change the ending." Her breathing grew ragged. "No." The word was barely a whisper, but it echoed louder than anything she had ever spoken. "No." Marisa's jaw clenched, her body trembling as her mind fought against the invisible chains that bound her to the chair. "I can't... I can't do this anymore."

Her vision sharpened as a flicker of clarity cut through the fog. This wasn't real. The blood. The deaths. The terror. None of it was real. "I have to let go." Her breath caught as a sudden wave of calm settled over her. "It's time." Marisa's eyes locked onto the chair—the root of everything. The power. The control. The prison.

Marisa stood, her legs weak beneath her as she backed away from the chair. It looked... ordinary. A worn antique. But Marisa knew better. It was a cage. Her mind spun as she grabbed the iron poker from the fireplace, her hands slick with sweat. "No more." Her voice was barely above a whisper as she gripped the poker tighter, her knuckles white. "You don't control me anymore." The air grew thick as Marisa raised the poker "I won't let you take me." She swung. The poker struck the chair's frame, splintering the wood with a loud crack that echoed through the room.

A violent ripple shook the air. The chair groaned, as if it were alive. "Again." Marisa's arms ached, but she didn't stop. She swung harder, her breath ragged as she struck again and again. The leather tore. The wood splintered. The air around her pulsed, thick with energy. Marisa's vision blurred, but she kept going. "I won't let you take me." Her pulse slammed in her ears as her muscles screamed. "I won't... let you... take me." With one final, desperate swing, the chair shattered.

Silence. Marisa's body felt... light. Her mind was blank, a vast emptiness where chaos had once lived. The chair was gone. But where was she? Her eyelids fluttered open, the harsh fluorescent lights burning her retinas. White. Everything was white. A dull ache throbbed at the base of her skull, her body heavy as if she had been asleep for an eternity. Marisa blinked, her vision adjusting as she stared up at the ceiling. "What...?" Her throat was dry, her voice barely a whisper. "She's awake." The voice was distant, muffled. Marisa's gaze shifted slowly, her head pounding as she took in her surroundings. A hospital room. The beeping of a heart monitor echoed softly beside her.

"Ms. Cole?" Her eyes struggled to focus as a nurse leaned over her, her expression soft but guarded. "You're safe now." "Where am I?" "You're in St. Roberts Psychiatric Hospital," the nurse said softly. Psychiatric hospital. Marisa's heart stopped. "No." The chair. Elias. The detective. The murder. "Was it real?" Her throat went dry, her vision blurring as the nurse's words echoed in her ears. "You've been here for a year, Ms. Cole." A year. Marisa's reality came crashing down.

"None of it was real?" The words slipped from Marisa's lips like air escaping a balloon—soft, deflated, broken. They barely reached her own ears, but the echo of the nurse's voice thundered in her mind. *"You've been experiencing a prolonged psychotic break, Ms. Cole. For over a year."* Her vision faltered, the sterile white walls of the room bending at the edges as if reality itself were struggling to stay in focus. Her heartbeat rang in her ears like a siren, and the fluorescent lights above buzzed with a sound that felt too loud, too sharp. Everything felt too sharp. "No..."

The floor seemed to drop out from under her. The bed beneath her back felt foreign, cold, like it belonged to someone else. Memories she had clung to—*Elias, the detective, the murder, the chair*—flashed through her mind in disjointed shards. Familiar faces turned to static. Events she could describe in vivid detail now unraveled like loose threads on a frayed page. A story. *Just* a story. One she had written herself. "What... what happened to me?" she whispered, as her throat closed around the words. The nurse's expression softened, but there was something off about her—something uncanny.

Her smile was a touch too practiced, her voice almost rehearsed, like someone playing a role they'd grown too comfortable in. Her uniform was immaculate, but her name badge had no name. Just a faded logo, half-rubbed away.

"After the success of your first book," the nurse said gently, "you... withdrew. The pressure. The expectations. The isolation. It was too much." Marisa tried to sit up, but her limbs were heavy, her body unwilling. Her skin tingled like it didn't quite belong to her. The room smelled like antiseptic. "Your mind created a world where you could escape," the nurse continued. "A place where you could control everything." Marisa's chest stiffened, and her breathing came faster, shorter, as if the very walls were leaning in to hear her unravel. "Elias never died?" she asked, the question catching in her throat. The nurse shook her head slowly, her eyes calm in a way that felt *wrong*. "He was never real."

The words hit like ice water down her spine. Her mouth opened, but no sound came. "And the detective?" she forced out. "A manifestation of your guilt," the nurse replied. "Your need for justice. For control. He was your mind trying to interrogate itself." Marisa's eyes filled with tears, her mind spinning like a wheel that had come loose from its track. "And the chair?" Her voice cracked. The nurse hesitated just a beat too long. Then, softer now: "The chair was never real either." She reached out, placing a cold, gloved hand over Marisa's. "We tell you this every day, Marisa. You just... don't remember."

Marisa stared at her, unblinking, the truth crashing over her in endless, suffocating waves. Her body sagged against the bed, all tension draining from her limbs as though her strings had been cut. Her vision blurred with tears. Her breath came in shudders. "None of it..." she whispered, voice trembling. Her head fell back against the pillow. The ceiling above her was white and endless. "None of it was real." And for the first time, she didn't know which version of her life hurt more—the one that never happened, or the one she was waking up in.

17

Twist of the Knife

The day Marisa Cole left St. Roberts Psychiatric Hospital, the sun was brighter than she remembered from 3 years ago. The air was crisp and cool, a soft breeze brushing against her skin as she stepped outside. Freedom. Real freedom. The weight that had suffocated her was gone. No more chair. No more stories. "You're really leaving this time, Ms. Cole," the nurse had said softly, her smile warm but cautious. "You're ready." Marisa had smiled, but the smile didn't quite reach her eyes. Was she ready? She wanted to be. "You're free now," she whispered to herself, feeling the sun's warmth on her skin. Her steps felt lighter as she walked toward the waiting car, her heart pounding. But deep down... Something was still there.

Her apartment looked exactly the same. Untouched. The bookshelves were still lined with her favorite novels. The smell of old paper and lavender candles lingered in the air. Too normal. Marisa's eyes scanned the room, her pulse raced as a familiar sense of unease stirred in her chest. "It's over," she whispered, her voice barely above a breath. But was it? Her fingertips grazed the edge of her writing desk, her eyes lingering on the spot where the chair had once been. The chair that wasn't real. Her throat tightened. "None of it was real." Marisa shook her head, forcing herself to breathe. "Move on." She walked to her bedroom, her steps slower now. Exhaustion weighed her down. A fresh start. That's what she needed. She pulled back the covers, ready to leave the past where it belonged. But as she turned toward her bed... Her heart stopped.

It was sitting on the chair by her bed. A small, leather-bound book. "No..." Her hands trembled as she stepped closer. Her eyes wide focusing on the muted, embossed title "Take Me Home. The same words. Her pulse pounded louder, her vision narrowing as memories flooded back. "Take me home." The words she had spoken in the chair to escape the worlds she created. "No... this isn't possible." Marisa's body went cold, her fingers trembling as she reached for the book. It felt... real. Too real. Her breath came in shallow gasps as she lifted it, the weight of it familiar and wrong. "It's just a coincidence." Her voice cracked as she tried to convince herself. But deep down, she knew. This wasn't over.

Marisa's fingers brushed over the smooth leather. "It's just a book." But her hands trembled as she opened it. The pages were filled with stories that she thought she had lived through. The past horrors that haunted her with The Detective and The Murder. The last page of the book was shocking. Marisa's eyes scanned the familiar handwriting. "You're not free yet, Marisa." Her pulse stopped. Her vision blurred as the words sank in, heavy and suffocating. "No..." "This can't be happening." Her mind spun, her thoughts unraveling as she stared at the haunting words. "You're not free." Her breathing grew shallow as the room tilted. "I destroyed the chair." Her voice was a trembling whisper, but the words felt hollow. "None of this is real." But... Was it?

Marisa stumbled back, her legs weak beneath her as the weight of the truth crashed down on her. "Did I... write this?" "Or was it written by someone else." "Did I leave this for myself... in case I ever got stuck again?" "Am I still... inside?" Her vision blurred as panic clawed at her chest. "No. No. NO." Her mind screamed against the possibility, but the weight in her chest told her otherwise. "What if I never left?" "What if..." Her pulse hammered harder as her eyes darted around the room. Everything looked the same. But was it? Her breathing grew faster, her hands trembling as she clutched the book. "What if I'm still in the chair?" Her thoughts spiraled, her mind splintering again. "Did I ever leave?"

Marisa's knees buckled as she sank onto the edge of her bed, her body trembling. "You're not free yet, Marisa." Her vision blurred as a chill ran down her spine. And then... She heard it. A whisper. Soft. Familiar. "Take me home." Marisa's breath caught as the words echoed softly around her. Her pulse stopped. She turned slowly. The chair was there. Back where it had always been. Waiting. Her blood turned to ice as her eyes locked onto it, her body frozen in place. "No..." The walls shivered. Reality tilted like a crooked painting sliding off its nail. Marisa's body shakes as the familiar, suffocating pull of the chair clawed at her. "It's not over."

Her breath came in ragged bursts, tearing from her throat like they didn't belong to her. She tried to move, to stand, to run—but her legs refused to listen. Her limbs felt heavy, sluggish, like they were no longer hers. Like the chair had already begun pulling her in. It was waiting. Still. Silent. Watching. The chair sat in the center of the room, its worn leather seat gleaming dully in the low light, the wood darker than she remembered, as if it had soaked in something it shouldn't have. It wasn't a piece of furniture anymore. It was a presence. A pulse. It breathed with her now. Waiting to take her home.

Her hands trembled violently as her gaze dropped to the book still clutched in her lap—its pages splayed open like a mouth mid-scream. She hadn't realized how tightly she was holding it, how *wrong* it felt. The weight of it wasn't right. It wasn't just paper. It was something *else*. She flipped to the last page, and the chill that swept through her didn't just crawl along her skin—it carved its way into her spine. There, at the very bottom, beneath the final line of text, in a handwriting she hadn't seen in over a decade—Daniel's signature. Her ex. Written in thick, black ink that looked wet—like it had just been scrawled, fresh and bleeding into the paper: "Take me home."

Marisa staggered back, the book tumbling from her hands and hitting the floor with a heavy, unnatural *thud*. The room began to warp, the walls pulsing as if the house itself had been holding its breath. *This wasn't her story.* It had never been. A scream rose in her throat, but it never escaped. Instead, fragments of forgotten memories ripped through her like glass—moments that hadn't made sense suddenly snapping into place. Daniel's voice, whispering behind her as she wrote. His notes in her margins, notes she never remembered writing. His edits. His ideas. His obsession. The chair wasn't a gift. It was a prison. *His* prison. Built from her mind, bound by his words.

Every twist. Every death. Every illusion of control—crafted by Daniel. He hadn't just influenced the story. He *had written it*. Word by word. Thought by thought. And now—she wasn't escaping his world. She had never *left* it. The floor beneath her creaked violently as if something stirred beneath it. The lights flickered. The air turned to ice. She turned back toward the chair, but it was no longer empty. Someone—or *something*—was sitting in it. Shadowy. Still. Watching her. Its outline looked almost familiar. Like a man. Like Daniel. The figure raised one hand, lazily, and pointed to the open book on the floor. A whisper filled the room, crawling into her ears from nowhere and everywhere at once:

"You're the story now, Marisa."

The last thing she saw before the room collapsed into darkness was the ink on the final page *moving*—letters shifting, rewriting themselves. Rewriting her. And the chair? It didn't wait anymore. It *took* her.

About the Author

Anthony Parson is a debut author, Emmy Award–winning sound designer, filmmaker, and Media Producer with the U.S. Army Field Band. Based in Richmond, Virginia, Anthony began his creative career in music studios, producing and engineering for artists before earning a bachelor's degree in Recording Arts from Full Sail University. It was during his time at Full Sail that Anthony's curiosity expanded beyond audio. While still in school, he began sitting in on film production classes, eventually lending his skills to short films—scoring, sound designing, and composing immersive soundscapes that elevated student projects into cinematic experiences.

Then came the camera. Then the scripts. Then the desire to tell stories in his own voice. His first short film, *Incoming Call*, became a turning point, leading him deeper into the world of narrative creation. In 2021, he earned an Emmy nomination for sound design, followed by a second nomination in 2022 for his documentary *Bateau On The James*. In 2023, he was awarded an Emmy for Best Sound Design for the short film *Treasure*, which he also wrote and produced.

Take Me Home marks Anthony's debut as a novelist. Originally conceived as a screenplay, the story outgrew the screen—it needed more space to explore the fragile boundaries between fiction, reality, and the human mind. Novels, he discovered, were the perfect place to explore those dark, emotional corners.

While Anthony transitions into fiction, he remains deeply rooted in film and music. His creative mission is clear: to tell immersive, mind-bending stories that transport readers, challenge perception, and shift perspectives. His work—across all mediums—centers on one goal: to make you feel something unforgettable.

www.ingramcontent.com/pod-product-compliance
Lightning Source LLC
Chambersburg PA
CBHW020647250626
47154CB00008B/2854